# A plea for help

I counted the plink of her tears as they dripped off her chin. Twenty-three. "Okay, Beulah, what do you want me to do?"

She wiped her eyes and looked at me. "I want you to find him before the coyotes get him."

"And why should I do that? I'm sure you're aware that he and I are rivals."

"Yes, I know, but the poor thing deserves another chance."

"Yeah? Well, so do I."

Our eyes met for a long moment, then she said, "If you can save him, you'll get your chance."

My ears shot up. "With you?" She nodded. "Wow, that's all I needed to hear! Which way did he go?"

"North, I think, toward the canyons. It will be dangerous."

"Dangerous? Ha! I can't even spell the word, so how could I be scared of it? I'm off on a mission, my little prairie flower. Later this afternoon, you and I will have important business to discuss."

# The Quest for the
# Great White Quail

## John R. Erickson

Illustrations by Gerald L. Holmes

PUFFIN BOOKS

$\overset{J}{\underset{\mathcal{E}}{\mathcal{E}}}\mathbf{ri}$

PUFFIN BOOKS

Published by the Penguin Group

Penguin Young Readers Group, 345 Hudson Street, New York, New York 10014, U.S.A.

Penguin Group (Canada), 90 Eglinton Avenue East, Suite 700, Toronto, Ontario,
Canada M4P 2Y3 (a division of Pearson Penguin Canada Inc.)

Penguin Books Ltd, 80 Strand, London WC2R 0RL, England

Penguin Ireland, 25 St Stephen's Green, Dublin 2, Ireland
(a division of Penguin Books Ltd)

Penguin Group (Australia), 250 Camberwell Road, Camberwell, Victoria 3124,
Australia (a division of Pearson Australia Group Pty Ltd)

Penguin Books India Pvt Ltd, 11 Community Centre,
Panchsheel Park, New Delhi - 110 017, India

Penguin Group (NZ), 67 Apollo Drive, Rosedale, North Shore. 0632,
New Zealand (a division of Pearson New Zealand Ltd)

Penguin Books (South Africa) (Pty) Ltd, 24 Sturdee Avenue,
Rosebank, Johannesburg 2196, South Africa

Registered Offices: Penguin Books Ltd, 80 Strand, London WC2R 0RL, England

Published simultaneously in the United States of America by Viking Children's
Books and Puffin Books, divisions of Penguin Young Readers Group, 2008

1 3 5 7 9 10 8 6 4 2

LIBRARY OF CONGRESS CATALOGING-IN-PUBLICATION DATA

Erickson, John R., 1943–
Hank the Cowdog : the quest for the Great White Quail / by John R. Erickson ;
illustrations by Gerald L. Holmes.    p. cm. — (Hank the Cowdog ; [52])
Summary: At the request of his beloved Beulah the collie, Hank the Cowdog
puts aside his urge to chew plastic and sets off in search of his nemesis,
Plato the wayward bird dog.

ISBN 978-0-14-241107-0 (pbk.) — ISBN 978-0-670-06338-3 (hardcover)

[1. Dogs—Fiction. 2. Ranch life—West (U.S.) —Fiction. 3. West (U.S.) —Fiction.
4. Humorous stories. 5. Mystery and detective stories.]
I. Holmes, Gerald L., ill. II. Title..
PZ7.E72556Hgq    2008    [Fic]—dc22    2007032248

Puffin Books ISBN 978-0-14-241107-0

Hank the Cowdog ® is a registered trademark of John R. Erickson.
Printed in the United States of America

*For George Clay IV,
in appreciation for all
the elk meat he didn't
share with me last fall*

# CONTENTS

# The Quest for the
# Great White Quail

HANK
THE COWDOG®

# CHAPTER ONE

# Drover Steals a Truck

It's me again, Hank the Cowdog. Some dogs get into trouble for compulsive behavior, did you know that?

The most common example comes from your bird-dog breeds. Bird dogs are famous for being . . . strange, let us say. One day they're living the good life with everything a dog could want, and the next day . . . poof, they're gone, off chasing a bird or who-knows-what. They're experts at getting lost and total dunces at finding their way back home, and that's only one of a hundred reasons why I've never had any use for bird dogs, especially Plato. More on him later.

But even some of your non-bird-dog breeds get

1

involved in compulsive behavior—chewing, for example. They see an object lying on the ground and some little voice in their mind says, "I've got to chew it!" If the object being chewed happens to be a stick or a bone, it seldom causes major problems, because . . . well, who cares about a stick or a bone? Nobody.

But these compulsions have a way of getting out of hand. Remember the wise old saying? Hmmm. I thought I remembered it, but all of a sudden . . . okay, let's skip the wise old saying. We don't need it anyway.

The point is that compulsive chewing is a bad habit that scores no points with our human friends. Our people don't like it when their worldly possessions get mauled by the family dog.

I knew that. What I didn't know, what I never would have dreamed, was that Drover had a chewing problem. It came to my attention on the morning of . . . I don't remember the day or the month, but it was some time in the warm months of the year.

I had been up most of the night, checking out a few Monster Reports and talking trash with the local coyotes. It's a little game we play. They come up to the edge of ranch headquarters and howl such things as, "Okay, man, we're going to raid your chicken house and steal all your chickens, and then we're gonna beat you up so bad, your own mother won't know your face!"

And I bark back a witty reply, such as, "Oh yeah? The last bum who tried that spent six weeks in Intensive Care. You want a piece of that, huh? You want a trip to the emergency room? Well, bring it on!"

That's pretty impressive, isn't it? You bet. Those guys don't get away with much on my outfit. The good news is that coyotes very seldom venture into ranch headquarters, so a dog is pretty safe mouthing off to them. Heh heh. It's fun, one of the little pleasures that make this job worthwhile.

Where were we? Oh yes, Drover. I had been up most of the night, patrolling ranch headquarters and whipping the daylights out of coyotes, and around eight o'clock in the morning I returned to my office in the Security Division's Vast Office Complex. Strolling into the office, I saw that my desk was piled high with reports, top secret files, satellite photos, and the latest briefing papers on enemy agents operating in my territory.

I was sifting through the stack of material, when I happened to glance to my right and saw

Drover. He was sitting on his gunnysack bed, chewing something and making unpleasant noises with his mouth and teeth. I looked closer and saw that he was chewing a plastic truck.

"What are you doing?"

"Fine, thanks, how about yourself?"

"You're chewing a truck, did you know that?"

He gave me a silly grin. "Oh yeah, but it's not a real truck."

"I know it's not a real truck."

"It's just a toy."

"I'm aware that it's just a toy. I'm also aware that it belongs to Little Alfred. In other words, you're chewing up one of his toys."

"No, I found it outside the yard. Alfred keeps his toys inside the yard, so it can't be his."

I marched over to him and gave him a stern glare. "Drover, have you lost your mind? Any toy truck you find on this ranch belongs to Little Alfred. Do you know why?"

He rolled his eyes around. "Well, let me think . . ."

"First, Slim and Loper drive real trucks and don't need cheap plastic imitations. Second, Sally May doesn't play with toys. And third, Baby Molly is a girl and doesn't care about trucks. Who or whom does that leave?"

"Well, let me think." He furrowed his brow. "Pete?"

I let out a groan. "Drover, Pete is a cat."

"Yeah, but he plays with things."

"He plays with his tail. Cats aren't smart enough to play with toys. Who's left?"

His head began to drift downward and his silly grin faded. "Well . . . gosh, I never would have chewed up a toy that belonged to Little Alfred."

"Yes, but that's exactly what you did. Look at your work."

He stared down at the truck, which had tooth tracks all over it. His lip began to quiver. "It looks pretty bad, now that you mention it."

"It looks awful, and I must tell you that I'm astonished by this burst of destructive behavior. We were hired to protect this ranch, Drover, not to chew it up."

A tear slid down his face. "Well, I couldn't help myself. I saw it and I just . . . I just had to chew it!"

I paced a few steps away and tried to plot my response. Getting mad, yelling, and fuming wouldn't accomplish anything. It was obvious that the runt had a problem. He needed counseling and, well, who could handle that job better than me?

I returned to his bedside. "Drover, you've

become a slave to your darker side. It's called Compulsive Chewing, and it's a serious problem."

He let out a wail. "Ohhh! I knew something was wrong! I'd never chewed up a truck in my whole life. What can I do?"

"You can do exactly what I tell you. If you follow my instructions, I think we can break this pattern of silly, destructive behavior."

He stared at me with pleading eyes. "Gosh, no fooling? There's hope?"

"Yes, but only if you're ready to seize control of your life and put this shabby episode behind you. Are you ready?" He gave his head a nod. "Good. Now listen carefully. First, you must repeat the Words of Healing."

"I don't remember the words."

"I haven't told you the words."

"Oh. Sorry."

"The words are—and please pay attention—the Words of Healing are as follows: 'Trucks are yucky, violets are blue/Anyone who'd chew one belongs in a zoo.'"

He gave me an empty stare. "That's all, just say the words?"

"That's correct, once before meals and twice at bedtime."

He frowned. "What if I forget the words?"

"Then the deal is off. You're on your own. It's your life, Drover, and you can either take control of it or let it spin out of control. If we don't get this thing stopped now, it'll only get worse."

He swallowed hard. "Well, I guess I can try."

"That's the spirit. Oh, and one more thing. For your own protection, I'll have to confiscate the truck." Suddenly, he grabbed up the truck in his mouth and turned away from me. "Drover, listen to me. You're showing all the symptoms of a full-blown case of Compulsive Chewing. You have to give it up."

There was a moment of tense silence, then the truck fell from his mouth. "It was the best truck I ever chewed."

"I know, but it's turned you into a maniac. Step aside." He moved out of the way. "You'll be glad, believe me."

"What'll you do with it?"

"I'll return it to the yard. If we're lucky, no one will ever suspect that you damaged the toy of an innocent child."

"I wish you wouldn't put it that way."

"But it's true, Drover. You see, that's what makes this disease so tragic. It causes dogs to steal from their best friends."

8

"Should I go with you?"

"Absolutely not. It might cause you to slide into a deadly relapse."

He stared at the ground and nodded his head. "I guess you're right. Better not take the chance."

I laid a paw on his shoulder. "Son, in a month or two, this will all be behind us and we can laugh about it. But today, I've got to get this thing out of here."

I snatched up the toy in my enormous jaws and hurried out of the office. The sooner I got rid of that thing, the better we would all be.

# CHAPTER TWO

# The Texas
# Bone Famine

I trotted past the garden, past Emerald Pond, up the hill north of the gas tanks, and to the front of the machine shed. There, I paused to reconoodle the situation down at the yard.

I didn't mind returning Drover's stolen property, but I sure didn't want to be observed by our people in the house. See, I had every reason to suppose that if they saw me with Alfred's truck in my mouth, they would assume that *I* was the one with the deadly Chewing Disorder. Even worse, they might accuse ME of being the thief.

It sounds crazy, doesn't it, the Head of Ranch Security being accused of chewing up toys, but let me remind you that such mistakes have happened before. Just when you think you've won their trust, they'll catch you in an awkward moment and start piling on the charges.

Sally May was the worst offender. I mean, there seemed to be no end to her suspicions. Did I need to add fuel to the fires of her suspicion? No sir, and that's why I did a Visual Sweep of the entire area: the west side of the house, the backyard, the porch, the flower beds, all the places where Sally May had been known to lurk.

I hate to put it that way—lurk—but after a dog's been nailed eight or ten times, after Sally May has suddenly appeared out of nowhere and caught him in an embarrassing situation, he gets a little punchy.

See, one of the valuable lessons I had learned about Sally May was that she often works at the kitchen sink. While peeling potatoes or washing dishes, she looks out the window and does surveillance of the backyard area. Just when you think the coast is clear and nobody is watching, she'll catch you in some little mistake. Then her voice will pierce the silence, causing every hair on your body to stand on end, and things start sliding downhill in a hurry. We sure didn't need any of that.

And, you know, the longer I thought about this deal, the less interested I was in getting blamed for Drover's crimes. What was in it for me? Nothing. But what would I do with the stolen property?

I submitted the problem to Heavy-Duty Analysis and arrived at a sensible solution. Instead of returning the truck to the yard, I would simply haul it off to a quiet spot and dump it. Somebody would find it eventually, and my name would never appear on anybody's list of suspects.

Great idea, and I was a little surprised that I hadn't thought of it sooner. I turned away from the house and trotted around to the north side of the machine shed. Once there, out of the view of prying eyes, I dropped the thing on the ground and heaved a big sigh of relief. At last, we were rid of it! Now I could get back to the business of . . .

I glanced around in a full circle. I didn't think that Drover had followed me, but you never know. His compulsion was very compulsive. I saw nothing and nobody, so I . . . uh . . . began staring at the toy truck. Why? Well, it's hard to explain to someone who's never been a dog, who's never experienced the . . .

How can I say this? Normal dogs sometimes

find themselves attracted to certain substances, don't you see, and notice that I said *normal* dogs. We're not talking about your perfect little do-right poodles and yip-yips that stay inside a house, wear perfume and ribbons, and never have a wayward thought.

We're talking about real dogs, normal, healthy, red-blooded American dogs that go to work every day, eat Co-op dog food out of a hubcap, and keep the country running. See, when a guy works eighteen hours a day, every once in a while he yearns for some entertainment. We're not talking about anything lavish or expensive, just simple pleasures that satisfy a tiny need, such as . . .

I found myself staring at the toy truck. It was a pretty shade of red and made of soft plastic, not the kind that breaks into splinters and hurts your teeth and gums. I could almost understand why Drover had been attracted to it. I mean, chewing soft plastic isn't the same as chewing a bone, but in times of bone shortages . . .

Did I mention that we were in the midst of a terrible Bone Famine? Maybe not, but we were. It was one of the longest, most brutal Bone Famines in recent memory. The supply of bones had just dried up, and dogs all over Texas had been forced to chew . . . well, other things. You know, sticks, rocks, newspapers, old shoes, and other things they wouldn't ordinarily chew.

I, uh, tossed glances over both shoulders and my eyes returned to the truck. I hadn't chewed a good bone in weeks . . . months . . . years, and all at once . . .

Okay, we need to talk. We're friends, right? We can talk about things that aren't necessarily pleasant, things we're not proud of? I'm just going to blurt it out.

I started chewing the truck, and I LOVED IT!

I had never dreamed that chewing plastic could be such an exciting experience, but it was, and all at once Drover didn't seem nearly as crazy as I'd thought.

I chewed it to smithereens and wanted more . . . more plastic! Yes, plastic. Who needs bones in a world full of nice chewy plastic? Bones can wear down your teeth and cause bone particles to collect in your estomagus, but plastic . . . it doesn't splinterize and poke your gums. Furthermore, since you don't swallow it, all the various pieces remain outside the bodily so-forth.

See, plastic was invented for DOGS. Maybe you didn't know that. Maybe I didn't know it either,

but after conducting this first experiment with a plastic substance, it became very clear to me that *someone out there had invented plastic so that dogs could chew it.*

Why not? For thousands of years, dogs have been man's best friend. We've liked our people when they were unlikable, loved them when they were unlovable, forgiven them when they were unforgivable. We've licked their ears when we really wanted ice cream, kept them warm on cold winter nights, laughed at their stale jokes, and listened to their corny songs about Old Paint and Dunny.

Don't we deserve something special? Yes, of course we do, and that special something is PLASTIC.

Okay, there's one little problem with plastic. Once chewed and re-chewed, it leaves a mess, but what's a little mess in the broader context of history? This world is a big place. Put the world on one side and a small deposit of shredded plastic on the other, and you can see right away that shredded plastic is no big deal. It's the kind of thing our people ought to ignore, right?

I'm glad you understand, because . . . well, once I had chewed up the truck, I found myself . . .

uh . . . wishing to find other objects made of plastic, shall we say.

I headed toward the house. As I was passing the front of the machine shed, I happened to notice the head of a small whitish dog peering out the crack between the two sliding doors. When I appeared on the scenery, the head vanished inside.

I stopped and stuck my head inside the door. "Drover? Come out. I know you're in there."

A moment later, he stepped out of the barn, and right away I picked up an important clue. He had twisted his body into the shape of a horseshoe and was flashing a goony smile. Maybe you've never seen such odd behavior in a dog, but I have. Drover does it fairly often, and it's a sign that he's feeling guilty about something.

"Why are you doing that?"

"Doing what?"

"You're moving around like . . . I don't know what. Like a donut that's had a bite taken out of it. Normal dogs walk in a straight line, Drover. You're walking like a crab."

"I'll be derned. I've never even seen a crab."

"Nevertheless, you're walking like a beached crab."

"I tried to eat a crawdad one time, but it bit me on the nose."

"Answer my question."

"I forgot. What did you ask?"

I stuck my nose into his face. "Why are you walking in that ridiculous manner? To tell you the truth, Drover, it embarrasses me to see you doing that."

His grin faded. "Well, I guess I'm feeling . . ."

"Yes? Yes? Finish your sentence. I'm a busy dog."

"I guess I'm feeling . . . guilty."

I gave him a triumphant smile. "Aha! I knew it. Drover, you should never try to conceal anything from me. I can read your thoughts like a duck out of water." I began pacing in front of him. "Okay, soldier, out with it. What have you done this time?"

"Well . . . what you said about Alfred's toy truck made me feel pretty bad."

"We've already discussed this. Why are you still brooding about it?"

"I started feeling this terrible burden of guilt, so I came up to the machine shed to hide. But you caught me."

"Are you sure you haven't done something

else? Look deeper into the darkness of your Inner Bean."

"No, it was the truck. It made me feel like a rat, messing up a kid's toy."

"Drover, that doesn't make sense. If you felt like a rat, why did you walk like a crab? Crabs and rats are not the same; therefore, they are very different."

"What's the difference?"

"Crabs bite."

"So do rats."

"That's exactly my point. They're completely different. Now, why are you still brooding over the toy truck?"

He stared at the ground. "Well, Alfred's out in the yard, looking for it. I thought you took it back."

"Huh? Well, of course I took it back."

"You've got something in your teeth."

"I beg your pardon?"

"I said, you've got something red in your teeth."

"Red? Don't be absurd." I whirled away from him and began scrubbing my teeth. "It must be some, uh, fragments of red meat."

"It looks kind of like plastic."

"It's red meat, Drover."

"I'll be derned. Where'd you get red meat?"

"Never mind where I got it."

"Wait. Maybe some of the plastic came off the truck when you were carrying it back to the gate."

I beamed him a pleasant smile. "There we go! Of course. Ha ha. Why didn't I think of that?"

"It's still there."

I scrubbed harder on my teeth. "How does it look now?"

He squinted his eyes. "You got it that time."

"Good, good. We certainly don't want to go around with dirty teeth, do we? Ha ha. No siree. Listen, how's your Chewing Disorder?"

He beamed a silly grin. "You know, it's much better. Those Words of Healing really helped."

"Great. Well, stick with the routine, son, and don't forget to brush your teeth." I lifted one ear and heard voices down at the house. "So Alfred can't find his truck, huh? I left it right there by the gate. Tell you what, I'll trot down there and help him out." I gave Drover a secret wink. "Kids."

"What's wrong with your eye?"

"What?"

"You've got a twitch in your eye."

I gave him a withering glare. "Nothing's wrong with my eye. I was giving you a secret wink so that we could share a little laugh about how kids are always misplacing their toys."

"Oh. Hee hee. Yeah, that was a good one."

"Just skip it, Drover, I'm sorry I mentioned it. Good-bye. I'm off to help a child in distress."

And with that, I left the dunce and went streaking down to the yard gate to, uh, help Alfred find his missing toy.

# The Dreaded She
# Appears

Alfred was standing outside the yard gate when I arrived in my patrol car. I screeched to a stop, switched off Sirens and Lights, and hurried to his side.

He wore a troubled expression, holding his chin with one hand (sometimes these little details are important) and frowning at the ground. He looked up and saw me, but he didn't smile.

"Hi, Hankie. I lost my twuck and I can't find it."

Instantly, I reached for the microphone of my mind and made an urgent call to Data Control. "DC, we've got a missing truck at the yard gate. Description: red plastic, a child's toy. Run a tracer on it. Over and out." I turned back to the boy and licked him on the face, just to let him know that, well, I had arrived on the scene and had taken charge of the case.

He pushed me away. "I was playing wiff it yesterday, right here by the gate, but now I can't find it."

I studied the ground in front of the gate. What I saw was a crime scene that had been muddled by unauthorized traffic: Alfred's sneaker tracks, a large boot print (probably Loper's), and a number of long parallel lines in the dust that appeared to be troy truck tracks . . . toy troy trucks . . . troy trick tracks . . .

Phooey. Let's back off and take another run at this. Toy. Truck. Tracks. There! That's kind of a toughie to say, isn't it? I'll bet you can't say it three times without getting your tang tungled . . . your tongue tangled, shall we say. Even I had a little trouble with it. Ha ha.

But the point is that the crime scene had been decaffeinated so badly that I couldn't make heads or toes of it. Whatever important clues might have been there had been lost. Going strictly on the evidence at hand, some ordinary mutt might have concluded that Alfred had stolen his own truck, but . . . well, that didn't make much sense.

I turned to the boy and switched my tail over to Slow Puzzled Wags, as if to say, "Well, that just

about wraps it up. The truck vanished into thin air, so let's just forget about it, huh?"

At that very moment, the back door opened and out stepped . . . yipes, it was HER. Sally May. The boy's mother and the lady of the house. "Did you find it, honey?"

Have we discussed Sally May? Yes, I'm sure we have, but let's go over it again. There is something about her that causes a dog to lower his eyes, drop his head, tuck his tail, and . . . well, start slinking away.

It's those EYES. They come at you like drill bits and bore their way into the dark corners of your mind. They're always suspicious, always looking for something. If you're a little boy, they're looking for a hair out of place or jelly stains in the corners of your mouth.

If you're a dog, the eyes are looking for *naughty thoughts*.

Fellers, if you have a naughty thought skipping around inside your mind, she'll know about it. How? We don't know. Science has no answer. It has something to do with motherhood. Some mothers seem to have this . . . this advanced form of radar, see, and it can pick up a naughty thought a mile away, even in the dead of night.

Nothing escapes those eyes. It's spooky. It's creepy. And it's enough to turn an honest, loyal dog into a nervous wreck.

She left the porch and came toward the gate, and I could feel her eyes walking into the private room of my mind, lifting all the rugs, checking every dark corner, and peering under every piece of furniture. And all at once . . .

You won't believe this, but before I knew it, I had . . . well, bent myself into the shape of a horse-shoe and was flashing her a loony grin, as if to say, "Hey, Sally May! Great to see you. How's the family, huh? Yard looks great. Is that a buzzard's nest you're wearing? Oops, your hair. Sorry. Anyway, Alfred and I were just . . . Boy, this weather's nice, isn't it?"

Okay, I had scolded Drover for bending himself into that ridiculous Horseshoe Position, but don't forget that I was standing in the glare of Sally May's eyes. She causes normal dogs to do crazy things, that's all I can say.

Did my groveling do any good? It was hard to tell. She scowled at me and said, "What's wrong with that dog?"

Alfred shrugged. "He's twying to be friendly, I guess."

"Well, he looks ridiculous. Hank, stop that!"

Huh? Okay, sure, you bet. I switched off Horseshoe and beamed her a smile of greatest sincerity. I even went to Broad Loving Wags on the tail section. She didn't notice. She was looking down at Alfred.

"You still can't find your truck? Honey, if you'd bring your toys inside at night, this wouldn't happen. When we put our things in their proper place, we can always find them."

"I know, Mom, but how could it just disappear?"

Her eyes swung around to . . . yipes . . . to me, and I began to melt. Did she know something? Had she been spying on me? Had Drover ratted on me? Don't forget, he'd said he felt like a RAT.

Suddenly a mysterious gravitational force seized my body and twisted it into the shape of a horseshoe again, and I felt a loony grin spreading across my mouth. I know, I know. I had already done this and it had only made her more irritable, but there are times when a dog isn't the mattress of his own face . . . master of his own fate, let us say. This appeared to be one of those times, and it seemed to make her even madder.

Her eyes widened and her nostrils flared out like the head of a rattlesnake and she screeched, "Will you stop that! What's wrong with you?"

I couldn't explain it. It was too deep and complicated, and don't forget that we dogs are limited to facial expressions and tail wags when we try to respond to our human friends. It isn't easy to say, "It's *you*! If you'll stop staring at me like a chicken hawk, I'll quit behaving like a chicken!"

I couldn't express these thoughts through tail wags. What's a poor dog to do when all his efforts to communicate with the lady of the house have ended in failure? I was at my whip's end . . . wit's end, let us say, so in one last desperate effort to soothe her ruffled feathers, I . . . well, I licked her on the ankle.

"Ahhhhhh!" She screamed and jumped backward, and now her eyes were flaming even wilder than before. "Don't lick me! I hate that!"

Huh? Okay, another bad idea. Some days, a guy just shouldn't get out of bed. If we depended on these people for our happiness and satisfaction, our lives would be pretty grim.

The good news is that she turned back to Little Alfred, letting me off the skewer of her eyes. "Honey, things don't just disappear. Your truck is somewhere in this yard, and you'll just have to hunt until you find it. I can't help you, because I have to feed the baby."

She turned and started back to the house. Whew! But then ... uh-oh ... she stopped, turned slowly around, and beamed her deadly laser-beam eyes directly at me.

Gulp. Now what?

In a low, menacing voice, she said, "I don't suppose YOU know anything about this, do you?"

HUH? Was she talking to me? I glanced around to see if she might be speaking to someone behind me. No luck there. No, it appeared that I was the target of her burning question, and I would have to come up with some kind of response.

In this moment of almost unbearable pressure, I decided to try Happy Dog. It had worked before, so maybe it would get me out of this crisis.

I cranked my lips upward into a broad smile, lifted my ears as high as they would go, thrashed my tail back and forth, and began jumping up and down. Taken all together, these gestures beamed her a message of hope and joy:

"Boy, what a beautiful day! Bright sunshine, clear sky, no wind. The birds are singing and flowers are blooming, and best of all, we have each other. And by golly, if we have each other in troubled times, well, what's missing? Nothing. We have it all, Sally May, and I'm sure you'll agree that we're all so happy, we couldn't be any happier. Right?"

I studied her face to see if it was selling. She rolled her eyes, muttered something under her breath, and walked into the house. When the door closed behind her, I dared to resume my normal breathing. Whew! Boy, that had been quite a storm, and you know, I never did figure out if Happy Dog had warmed her heart or not.

Probably not. It might have caused some melting of the outer layers, but the deeper permafrost regions remained as cold as ever. Oh well.

I turned to Little Alfred and was saddened to see that he was giving me a suspicious look. "Hankie, you didn't take my twuck, did you?"

Huh? Me? Take his twuck? Heck no, honest. I could say, with a perfectly clear conscience, that I had never even seen a *twuck* in my whole life. I'd seen a few *trucks*, even a few toy trucks, but that's not what he'd asked about. No, I knew nothing, almost nothing at all, about his missing twuck. No kidding.

He smiled and gave me . . . arg . . . a big hug, such a loving embrace that it cut off the flow of carbon de angelo to my lungalary region and caused me to cough. HARK. And he said, "You wouldn't steal my twuck, Hankie, I know you wouldn't."

There, you see? When we want to get to the truth of any situation, we should ask the opinion of an innocent child. They don't lie or spread vicious gossip. Out of the mouth of Sally May's adorable child, I had been cleared of all charges.

It was just a pity that his mother wasn't around to hear the verdict.

# We Search for
# the Missing Twuck

Pretty touching scene, huh? You bet. A boy and his dog. It's one of the most special relationships in the whole world, two different creatures whose souls are joined at the center. The rest of the world could go on fighting and bickering, but Alfred and I . . . well, we had a bond of trust and friendship that would make us pals forever.

Should I lick him on the ear to seal the friendship? I pondered that for a moment. The last time I'd licked him, he'd pushed me away. And when I'd licked his mother on the ankle, she had recoiled in horror, as though she'd been bitten by a snake.

Sometimes those licks work and sometimes they don't. I decided to save it for another time.

Alfred released me from his hug and his face settled into a mask of wrinkles. "Hankie, I want to play twucks. Will you help me find my twuck?"

Me? Oh, sure, you bet. Anything at all. Be glad to help.

He walked through the open gate. "Well, wet's check the yard."

Huh? The yard? Now, hold on a second. It was a well-known fact that his mother had strict rules about Dogs in the Yard. I had just come through a narrow escape with that woman and I wasn't anxious to push my luck. No thanks.

He stopped and looked back at me. "It's okay. Mom's feeding Molly and she won't notice." He flashed a grin. "Molly likes to spit out her food and Mom'll be busy wiping up the mess."

Yeah? Well, to be perfectly frank, it made me a little uneasy to bet my life on whether or not a little girl-child spitted out her food. Spat. Sput.

"Come on, Hankie, I need your help."

I turned my gaze toward the house to see if The Face was lurking at the kitchen window, looking outside for lawbreakers. The window was clear, so . . . okay, maybe we had time for a quick search of the yard, although I had serious doubts that we would find the, uh, twuck.

I slipped through the gate and entered the

33

Forbidden Zone, and right away I could feel the tension moving over me. My mouth seemed very dry, and I noticed that my left eye had begun to twitch.

You see what she does to me? I was in the yard to help her son find his toy, yet her dark presence hovered over the place like . . . something. Like the smoke from a thousand burning tires.

We made one quick pass around the yard, front and back, and our search turned up no sign of the missing twuck. It was discouraging, although it came as no surprise . . . that is, we were both pretty discouraged. At that point, Alfred changed the plan of attack. We would now do a thorough search of all plants, flowers, bushes, and shrubberies.

Aye, captain! I activated Snifforadar, put my sensors down to ground level, and began sweeping the dense foliage that grew in the flower beds next to the house. I checked out a clump of bazoonias just north of the porch and continued on a northward course of 0400, following the foundation line of the house. Snifforadar was operating at the maximum level and showing nothing on the scope, so I crept onward until . . .

BAM!

Aaaa-eeeeee!

Holy smokes, in the heat of the search, it had never occurred to me that a huge and deadly rattlesnake might be coiled up beneath the shrubberies, waiting to pounce on a passing mouse. Or a rabbit. Maybe even a stray goat, sheep, or cow— I mean, we're talking about a snake that was big enough to swallow a half-grown cow!

Huge snake, and I hate to be the one to give you the bad news, but the snake had made a direct hit with two Fang Missiles, right on the soft leathery portion of my nose.

I guess you know what this means. It means that our story might turn out to be shorter than we'd planned. We've discussed rattlesnakes, right? We know what their deadly venom can do once it's been injected into the living tissue of a dog, and we also know that the very worse place for a dog to be bitten is on the end of his nose.

Alfred heard my cries of pain and came rushing over to me. By then, the deadly poison had already begun racing through my bodily processes and I was feeling faint. I staggered toward the boy, looked into his eyes, and delivered the terrible news:

"Son, we've taken a direct hit and things are

looking bad. By some estimates, we've got maybe one hour to rush me to the Mayo Clinic. As much as I hate to say this, we're going to have to sound the alarm, alert your mother, and tell her to put in an urgent call for a Medivac helicopter. They fly out of Amarillo, so we don't have a moment to spare."

The boy narrowed his eyes and looked at the end of my nose.

"Uh . . . Alfred, I don't want to rush you, but . . . yes I do! Don't just stand there looking at my nose! The clock is running and I can feel the poison spreading through my body. Fifty-five minutes, that's all we have left. Hurry, call your mother!"

Why was he grinning? Was there something funny about the family dog being attacked by an eight-foot diamondback rattlesnake? Hey, I'd gotten a good look at the thing, and he was at least ten feet long, biggest snake I'd ever seen.

What? He was laughing now! "Hankie, did Pete scratch your nose?"

I stared at him in disbelief. PETE? Was I dumb? Was I blind? Didn't I know the difference between a shrimpy little ranch cat and an enormous rattlesnake? Pete had nothing to do with it.

I'd been attacked by . . . I turned toward the bush and pointed my throbbing nose toward . . .

HUH?

Okay, let's relax a moment and try to, uh, put this all together. Tension does strange things to a dog's mind, to everyone's mind actually, and if you'll remember, we had been working under a heavy load of tension. Sometimes a guy's mind gets so focused on the work at hand . . . sometimes the burden of tension grows so heavy . . .

Phooey. You've probably figured it out anyway. Okay, maybe it was the cat, but let me hasten to point out that snakes often crawl into the yard and lie in the shade of bushes and shrubberies, and if a dog ever stuck his nose into one of those . . .

I whirled away from Alfred and stormed over to the cat. "Idiot! You just slapped me across the nose!"

I glared into the face of my least-favorite character on the ranch, in the entire world. Pete the Barncat. He was smirking, of course. He always smirks, and it drives me nuts.

He fluttered his eyelashes. "Well, Hankie, don't stick your nose where it doesn't belong."

I stuck my nose right in his face. "I'll put my

nose . . ." BAM! Tears of pain rushed to my eyes, causing Pete's face to swim out of focus. "You just slapped me again!"

"I know, Hankie. Want to try for three in a row?"

Would I fall for this trick? Yes, by George, and do you know why? Because I had a right to stick my nose anywhere I . . .

BAM!

. . . wanted. And having made my point, I withdrew from the field of battle, so to speak, and walked back to Little Alfred. I went to Short Rapid Wags on the tail section and beamed him an earnest look that said, "Alfred, your mother's cat is out of control. I was just trying to be friendly and the little snot slugged me—three times! It was an unprovoked attack and I wish you'd . . ."

I stormed back to the cat. "Pete, I was conducting an important search of the yard and trying to help this boy find his lost truck. But do you care about children? Do you care about anyone but yourself? Pete, you make me sick!"

He drummed his claws on the ground and stared at me with his weird yellow eyes. "Hankie, if you push this, I'll yowl and screech, and guess who will come flying out of the house with her broom."

I glared daggers at the little pestilence. Since there was more than a shred of truth in his pack of lies, I, uh, decided to soften my tone and take the Road of Maturity.

"Pete, there's no need for that. It's a sad day when the citizens of this ranch can't get along with each other."

He heaved a sigh and turned his gaze up toward the sky. "Hankie, there's a very simple solution to this. Leave my yard and we'll get along fine."

"Your yard? This is *your* yard now? Ha ha!"

He grinned and nodded his head. "Um hm. Or if you'd rather, I can call Sally May and we'll let her handle it."

The laughter died in my throat. "Okay, kitty, you're holding the high cards this time, but don't think . . ."

, "Good-bye, Hankie."

"Don't think you've heard the last of this. I'll come back, and when I do, Sally May won't be around to save your skin." With that stinging reply, I whirled around and marched away, leaving the cat in the shambles of his own ruins.

# The Milk Jug
# Episode

Holding my head at a proud angle, I stormed away from the cat and headed straight for the gate. There, I caught sight of something out of the cornea of my eye. I stopped and took a closer look: Sally May's garden trowel with a red plastic handle was sitting beside the fence.

*Plastic!* My mouth began to water and I had to send out my tongue to mop up several drips. I'd never chewed a garden trowel before, but all at once my enormous jaws closed around the plastic handle. I was about to go sprinting away from the scene of the scenery, when suddenly my blood was frozen by a voice.

"HANK! Put down my trowel!"

Huh? Was that the voice of the Dreaded She? I cut my eyes from side to side and lifted both ears to Full Gathering Position.

The voice came again: "And get out of my yard! Now!"

There, you see! What did I tell you? The woman never sleeps, never closes her eyes, never shuts down her radar.

"Alfred, get my trowel away from that nincompoop before he chews it up!"

Nincompoop? This was an outrage! Once again, she had witnessed only the tip of the ice cube and had rushed to judgment, accusing me of a crime I hadn't committed yet or even thought about committing.

Okay, maybe I'd thought about it, but there's no crime in thinking about a crime. By George, this is still America!

Little Alfred came trotting around the side of the house, heading toward me. I began flipping switches on the console of my mind, activating Slow Wags, Wounded Eyes, and Dispirited Ears.

"Hankie, that's my mom's shovel and you can't have it." He seized the trowel and tried to snatch it out of my mouth.

You know, if he'd asked nicely or shown any

interest in reaching some kind of negotiated settlement, I would have gone for the deal, but when he grabbed it . . . well, I just acted on impulse. I held on tighter. He jerked and I jerked back. And all at once, things got out of hand. The harder he pulled, the more determined I was to hang on.

"Hankie, give it to me!"

It's sad when old friends get sucked into ugly confrontations, but I wasn't ready to give up the trowel, and I, well, snatched it out of his hands and made a dash for the machine shed.

Behind me, I heard him wail, "Mom, he took your shovel!"

"HANK!"

Okay, forget the stupid trowel. I dropped it and sprinted up to the machine shed. It wasn't worth a confrontation with Sally May and her broom. She and I had enough problems without getting into a fight over a silly little garden tool.

I had planned to take refuge in the machine shed but decided not to. Drover would be there and I had no interest in spending any more time with him, so I headed for the shelter belt, just north of the machine shed. There, hiding behind a line of cedar trees, I was alone with my thoughts and could . . .

Hmmm. It appeared that a plastic milk jug had blown out of the garbage barrel and lodged itself against the trunk of one of the cedar trees. Was this just a random event or did it point to some deeper pattern in the universe? I mean, plastic milk jugs are made of plastic, right? And plastic had become a major issue in my life, and all at once it seemed perfectly clear . . .

I glanced over both shoulders, just to be sure that I was alone, and began . . . well, chewing the milk carton. Why not? It didn't belong to anyone and, by George, *I wanted to chew some plastic.*

"Oh, hi. What are you doing?"

Huh? I froze and spit several pieces of plastic out of my mouth. Slowly, I turned my head and saw . . . Drover. "I'm doing nothing, and even if I were, it wouldn't be any of your business."

"I'll be derned. There for a second, I thought you were chewing plastic . . . or something."

"Once again, Drover, you have taken a tiny shred of data and pumped it up into a wild generalization."

"Yeah, but I see shreds of plastic, and that makes me think you might be . . . well, sort of shredding up the milk carton."

"With only three shreds of evidence, you're

going to leap to the conclusion that I'm chewing plastic? Is that what you're saying?"

"Well . . . I wondered."

I cut my eyes from side to side. My mind was racing. "All right, you little snoop, maybe I'm chewing a milk jug. I'm out of bones and I don't chew wood. What's a dog supposed to do in his spare time?"

"Well, you told me . . ."

"Drover, I told you that it was wrong to chew up children's toys. I said nothing about milk cartons. It's an entirely different situation."

"Yeah, but somebody chewed up Little Alfred's truck, too. I just saw the pieces, right over there behind the machine shed, and I didn't do it."

Those words sent a jolt down my spine. "What? Are you serious? Why wasn't I informed of this? Come on, son, we need to check this out!" We rushed over to the north side of the machine shed and, sure enough, there were the ruins of Alfred's truck, two hundred pieces of red plastic.

I studied the evidence. "I'm seeing a pattern here. Notice the size of the tooth marks?"

"Yeah, they're pretty big."

"They're very small, Drover. Whoever did this had small spiky teeth. Hmmm. What sort of animal has small spiky teeth? Wait! Cats have small spiky teeth. We're making progress, son. Can you think of any cats who might have done this?"

He gave me a blank stare. "Well . . . I know a cat, but I don't think those tooth marks came from a cat."

I stared at him in astonishment. "What?"

"They're too big. They look more like . . . dog teeth."

I marched over to one of the fragments and gave it a closer inspection. "Hmm. You've got a point. Those puncture holes do indeed match the ballistics of dog teeth." I drifted a few steps away and gazed off into the distance. "Drover, this case has taken a sudden turn for the worse. The shadow of suspicion has fallen upon someone we know."

"Yeah, that's what I was thinking."

I whirled around and faced him. "I never would have dreamed *you* would do such a thing!"

His eyes bugged out. "Me! I thought it was you!"

I began pacing a circle around him, a technique I often use when I'm interrogating a reluctness witling . . . a reluctant witness, let us say. "Consider the evidence, Drover. Those plastic fragments show the marks of dog teeth. Are you a dog?"

"Well . . . yes."

"And tell this court, do you have teeth in your mouth?"

"Well . . . I guess so."

"Therefore, we have established that you have in your possession the very weapon that was used in this crime: dog teeth! Is that correct?"

"Yeah, but . . ."

"And tell this court who stole the truck in the first place. And who was suffering from an out-of-control Chewing Disorder?"

The force of my interrogation had reduced him to jelly. He collapsed into a pile and let out a groan. "I didn't do it! Honest, I didn't do it!"

I strolled over to him and beamed him a look of righteous anger. "Drover, the mark of a crook is that he always denies his guilt. If you had told this court that you were guilty, we would have known that you were innocent."

"All right then! I did it!"

A cunning smile rippled across my mouth. "No further questions, your honor. The witness has admitted his guilt."

His head shot up and he stared at me with wide eyes. "Yeah, but I didn't do it!"

"Well, that's too bad because you've already confessed. This court is now adjourned."

I walked away from him, proud that I had won the case. But then I heard him say, "Hank, you did it and that's why Little Alfred couldn't find his truck. You chewed it to smithereens, didn't you? Tell the truth."

Tell the truth. Drover's words hung in the air like buzzards and for several throbbing moments, our eyes were locked in a deadly struggle. Thoughts raced through my mind until, all at once, it was clear to me what I had to do: *beat him up*. My lips curled into snarl, my eyes narrowed into slits, I moved toward him like a bulldozer, and . . .

I stopped. My head sank. "All right, you little squeakbox, now you know my darkest secrets."

"So . . . you really did it?"

"Of course I did it! Furthermore, I enjoyed every second of it and I absolutely love chewing plastic."

"Uh-oh."

"Right. Uh-oh. It seems that I've developed an incurable lust for plastic, and I caught it from *you*!" Again, I began pacing. "Drover, all my life I've seen objects made of plastic and had no interest in them, none. But then you showed up

**49**

with that plastic truck and started gnawing on it and . . . look what you've done to me!"

His lower lip trembled. "So it's my fault?"

"Of course it's your fault! Chewing plastic is the dumbest thing I ever heard of. On my own, I never would have thought of doing it."

"Yeah, but you did."

"I did, Drover, because you did it first."

"Yeah, but I quit. Maybe you should quit."

I stopped in my trucks . . . stopped in my tracks, let us say, and turned to face him. "Quit? Is that what you said?" I marched back to him. "That's crazy! Don't you get it? I *love* chewing plastic, and love is what makes this world go 'round. Do you want the world to stop going around?"

"Well . . ."

"Drover, if the world suddenly stopped spinning on its axels, birds would be thrown out of trees. Clouds would crash into each other. The machine shed would fall into splinters, our dog-food bowl would go flying all the way to China, and we would starve. Is that what you want?"

He shook his head and let out a moan. "I'm so confused, I don't know what to think!"

"Well, quitting plastic is not the answer."

"Yeah, but what is?"

There was a long moment of silence as each of us tried to deal with this crisis. At last I said, "I have a suggestion. I won't tell anyone you stole the truck if you won't tell anyone I ate it."

"I guess that'll work."

"Good. Now, regarding the milk carton . . . let's chew it together. If we're going to be afflickened with a Chewing Disorder, at least we can do it as a team and celebrate the joy of behaving like lunatics."

"Yeah, but I already quit."

"Well, un-quit. Good habits are hard to break, but it can be done."

He blinked his eyes and smiled. "You really think so?"

I marched over to him and placed a paw on his shoulder. "I'm sure of it, son. It won't be easy, but I'll be right beside you every step of the way. If you need a shoulder to lean on, I'll be here."

His smile widened and he fluttered his stub tail. "You know, I think I can do it!"

"That's the spirit. Drover, I'm proud of you. Come on, let's chew some plastic!"

And with that, we indulged ourselves in one of the joys of being a dog, chewing a plastic milk jug into a thousand pieces.

# Miss Beulah
# Pays Me a Call

B oy, you should have seen us! We jumped into the middle of that milk carton and had ourselves a blast. We tore and chewed and spit, then did it all over again, until we had reduced the carton to shreds. At that point, we stood together, two proud members of the Security Division Elite Guards, admiring our work.

"Well, what do you think, Drover, was that fun or what?"

"Yeah, I can't believe I ever gave up plastic."

"Yes, well, this is just the beginning, son. There's more where that came from. In fact, I'll tell you a secret. Just a while ago, I spotted an awesome garden trowel in the yard."

His eyes blanked out. "Yeah, but I don't eat shovels."

"No, no, not the shovel part. It has a plastic handle, see, red plastic that's just as soft and chewy as . . ." I noticed that his gaze had wandered toward something in the distance. "Are you listening?"

"Oh my gosh! It's Miss Beulah!"

HUH?

Miss Beulah, on our ranch? That was impossible. She wasn't the kind of dog who strayed off her own place. Furthermore, she had never paid us a visit by herself, never.

"Drover, you need to get your eyes checked. I don't know what you're seeing out there, but . . ."

"It's a lady dog."

"It may be a lady dog, son, but I can promise you . . ." I turned my gaze toward the northeast and . . . hmmm, saw what appeared to be an unidentified dog some three hundred yards away, coming in our direction. And the evidence suggested that she might be of the female variety. "Okay, maybe it's a lady dog, but . . ."

"Oh my gosh, I think I'm in love!" ZOOM! In a flash, he was gone, running toward the stranger.

"Drover, come back here! It's not Miss Beulah,

and you're not in love. Drover, I'm ordering you to stop!"

There was no calling him back. The runt seemed to have lost what little mind he had left and was streaking toward the stranger. Whoever that was out there would get her first impression of our ranch by meeting Drover, and that would be a terrible shock.

I narrowed my eyes and looked closer. Drover had reached the stranger, and now he was ... well, hopping like a grasshopper and rolling around on the grass, almost as though ... I had seen this type of behavior before, and it became obvious that I needed to check things out myself.

I went ripping out into the pasture to save the lady-stranger from the shock of meeting Drover, when all at once I noticed that I was ... well, hopping up and down, diving through the air, and doing rolls in the grass. Do you see the meaning of this?

Okay, it really *was* Miss Beulah and that explained all the ... uh ... odd behavior in the ranks of the Security Division's greeting committee. We've discussed Miss Beulah, right? Long collie nose, flaxen hair, gorgeous brown eyes, and a perfect set of ears.

She was the one true love of my life. Many a night had she visited my dreams, but never had she been so bold as to visit me in person . . . at least, not all by herself!

See, there had always been a bird dog in her life, a stick-tailed half-wit named Plato. I had never understood what she saw in a guy who chased birds and fetched tennis shoes, but now it appeared that she had finally come to her senses.

SHE HAD COME TO ME!

I rushed up to her and would have flown into her arms, only Drover had gotten there first and was making a complete fool of himself. "Oh, Miss Beulah . . . roses are red and cornmeal is grainy/ Your beautiful face just drives me insaney!"

"Drover, please control yourself!"

He didn't miss a beat, but took a deep breath and fired off another silly poem. "I've read about roses, they made me feel blue/'Cause violet roses remind me of you."

"Drover, that's outrageous! You'll do anything to make a rhyme. There's no such thing as a violet rose and besides . . ." I shoved him out of the way and looked into the face that had launched a thousand poems, and from my lips there floweth an astounding piece of literature:

I knew when I saw you that this was the end
Of Plato's involvement with you as a friend.

I'll tell you quite frankly, I've thought
    many times,
You could have had dollars but settled
    for dimes.

But Plato is gone, not a minute too soon,
At last you have ditched your bird-dog
    buffoon!

I gazed up into her lovely face to see if my
poem had absolutely swept her away, but Drover
came blundering back onto the stage, spouting
another piece of ragged nonsense:

Oh Beulah, my heart rate has gone off
    the scale.
My blood pressure's rising, my face has
    turned pale.
My vision's so blurry, I hardly can see.
My kidneys are pumping so hard, I might . . .

Now get this. The little mutt's eyes popped
wide open and crossed. He let out a gasp and said,
"Uh-oh!" In a flash, he left and scampered behind
a wild plum thicket nearby.

Well, he should have known better than to get into a Poetry Fight with me. Words have power and meaning, you know, and mutts who aren't trained to handle powerful love poems can get themselves into trouble.

I could have warned him, but he wouldn't have listened. When Beulah enters the scene, he comes unhinged, loses all touch with reality, and thinks . . . I don't know, that he's some world-famous poet, but he's not even close.

Well, with Drover out of the contest, I swung my gaze around and feasted my eyes on . . . huh? She had turned away and seemed to be . . . well, crying. I rushed to her side.

"Miss Beulah, as Head of the Security Division, I want to issue a formal apology for Drover's shameful behavior. We've known for a long time that he writes gawky poems, but we never dreamed that he would inflict his shabby doggerel on such a fine lady as yourself. On behalf of the entire Security Division, I want you to know that we're shocked and embarrassed."

She shook her head. "It wasn't Drover."

"Huh? Of course it was Drover. The other poetry you heard was of the highest quality, and you might have noticed that . . . well, I wrote it myself. Just for you, by the way, and I hope you paid special attention to the rhymes. Perfect rhymes, Beulah, every line handmade in the workshop of my heart."

Again, she shook her head. "Your poem was sweet. Thank you."

"Well, then what's the problem?"

"I've made a fool of myself, coming here... oh, you wouldn't understand!"

She hurried away. What was going on around here? I ran after her and stood in her path, forcing her to stop. "Beulah, you can't show up on my ranch, burst into tears, and then just walk away. Has Plato said something to make you cry? Because if he has ..."

She shook her head. "No, it's nothing like that." She brushed a tear out of her eye and looked at me. "Hank, it was foolish of me to come here. This isn't your problem."

"Beulah, anything that makes you cry is my problem. Tell me, and hurry before the Prince of Rhymes comes back and starts spouting nonsense."

She heaved a sigh and looked off into the distance. "It's Plato. He's wandered off again, looking for quail."

"No kidding? Hey, that's the best news I've heard in months! Congratulations, my little sugar plum! Maybe this time, he'll stay gone forever."

She whirled around and faced me with a pair of flaming eyes. "See? I knew this would be a waste of time, I knew you wouldn't . . ." She burst into tears again.

Well, gee, what's a guy supposed to say? I mean, she had just delivered a great piece of news and had made me the happiest dog in Texas, and now she was bawling. Did that make sense? No, but Beulah had always been a little hard to figure out.

I gave her a moment to get control of herself. "All right, Beulah, go on. I'll listen."

She took a deep breath and walked a few steps away. "Plato is a bird dog, and bird dogs are . . . they have a peculiar side."

"Beulah, I am so glad to hear you say that, and if I might expand . . ."

"Hank! You said you would listen."

"Oh. Yes. Sorry."

"Bird dogs are hunters, and when quail season is over, they sometimes get restless. All their instincts and energy and training have no place to go. The poor dear has tried to keep himself occupied, pointing his tennis shoe and fetching . . . well, everything on the place that wasn't tied down, but it wasn't enough. Four days ago, I noticed an odd look in his eyes. He was staring off into space."

I let out a groan. "Oh great! Let me guess. The birdbrain wandered off the ranch and can't find his way back home?"

She nodded. "Yes, but it's worse than that. This is the third time in two weeks and Billy, our master, is tired of driving all over the country to look for him."

This sent a pleasant tingle rushing down my spine. "Gee, that's too bad. I mean, in some ways he was a pleasant jerk."

She glared at me. "He's better than you'll ever know. He's kind, considerate, and loyal, the sweetest dog I've ever known." Her lip trembled. "But he has this other side. He gets so silly sometimes and I'm afraid . . ." She turned away and the tears flowed.

I counted the plink of her tears as they dripped off her chin. Twenty-three. "Okay, Beulah, what do you want me to do?"

She wiped her eyes and looked at me. "I want you to find him before the coyotes get him."

"And why should I do that? I'm sure you're aware that he and I are rivals."

"Yes, I know, but the poor thing deserves another chance."

"Yeah? Well, so do I."

Our eyes met for a long moment, then she said, "If you can save him, you'll get your chance."

My ears shot up. "With you?" She nodded. "Wow, that's all I needed to hear! Which way did he go?"

"North, I think, toward the canyons. It will be dangerous."

"Dangerous? Ha! I can't even spell the word, so how could I be scared of it? I'm off on a mission, my little prairie flower. Later this afternoon, you and I will have important business to discuss."

"Just save him, Hank, that's all that matters."

I gave her a kiss on the cheek. "That's *not* all that matters, but it's a place to start. Good-bye, Miss Beulah!"

And with that, I went streaking off to the north to begin a Search and Rescue Mission for a guy who didn't deserve it.

# CHAPTER SEVEN

# Drover Is Injured
# in the Line of Duty

I hadn't planned on taking Little Shakespeare on the mission, but when he finished his business in the plum thicket and saw me streaking away, he figured out that something was afoot, and he came scampering after me.

"Hank, wait up! Where are we going?"

"We? *We* aren't going anywhere, you little buttinski, but *I'm* going out on an important mission."

"Oh goodie, how fun! Can I go?"

I slowed down to a walk. "Absolutely not."

"Gosh, how come?"

I stopped and gave him a scorching glare. "Drover, after that incident with Miss Beulah, I'm

**63**

ashamed to be seen with you. You've brought disgrace to the entire Security Division."

"Gee, all I did was . . ."

"Furthermore, you tried to steal my girl with cheap tricks and mawkish poems."

"I thought they were pretty good."

"They were dreadful. That last poem you did, the one about blood pressure and kidneys . . . Drover, it sounded like an autopsy report!"

"Yeah, but she liked it."

"She hated it. And then, right in the middle of your presentation, what did you do?"

"Well . . ."

"You ran to the bathroom!"

"It was a plum bush."

"Drover, I knew what you were doing, and so did Beulah."

His head sank. "You really think so?"

"Of course she knew. Everybody knew."

"She didn't laugh, did she?"

"You didn't hear? Drover, she laughed her head off!"

"I thought she was crying."

"She laughed until she cried. Does that make you proud of yourself?"

He let out a groan and fell to the ground. "I

couldn't help it, I had to go! Oh, I'm so embarrassed! I'll never be able to face her again."

He moaned and blubbered for, oh, three minutes at least, until I said, "Get up, son, you've suffered enough." He didn't budge. "Drover, you can't punish yourself forever, just because you . . . well, behaved like an idiot."

"Yes, I can! I'm going to stay here forever!"

"Drover, every cloud has a silver lining, but I must remind you that you're not a cloud."

He peeked up at me. "I'm not?"

"You're a dog. You'll always be a dog, and you'll never be a cloud. Are you feeling better now?"

"Not really."

I whopped him on the back. "Good! Now, let's get out of here, we've got work to do."

I trotted off to the north, and he caught up with me. "I thought you said I couldn't go."

"I changed my mind. After all the suffering you've done, you deserve a promotion."

His eyes lit up. "No fooling? Gosh, thanks! A real promotion, how neat! What am I going to do?"

"We're going to be traveling through coyote-infested canyons, and I thought we might let you go out on a scout patrol."

All at once, he stumbled and let out a yell.

"Help! Get out of the way!" Before my very eyes, he nosed into the ground and did four forward rolls.

When he had rolled to a stop, I rushed to his side and coughed on the cloud of dust he had kicked up. "What happened?"

"Blowout, left front leg!"

"That was a bad wreck. Are you all right?"

"Oh yeah, and I've got to carry on with the mission. I'll be fine." He struggled to his feet, hobbled three steps, and collapsed. "Oh darn, there it went again! Help me up, I've got to keep going!"

This was definitely a new Drover, one we had never seen before. I was proud of the little mutt. "All right, men, forward march! To the canyons!" As we marched northward, I watched him. I could see lines of pain etched on his face. "How are you doing, trooper?"

"I'm not going to quit. I've been promoted to Scout."

We marched on. His limp grew worse. "Drover, if it gets unbearable, we can halt the column and rest."

"Never! I'll eat the pain for breakfast."

We continued the march, but after we had gone another hundred yards, I could see that he

was in agony, lurching along and weaving from side to side, his burning eyes locked on the distant horizon.

At last I halted the column. "Drover, I can't let you go on like this."

He turned to me with a crazy, fevered stare. "Got to go on! Turn me loose!"

To my astonishment, he jerked away from the grisp of my grasp, staggered three more steps and crashed to the ground. I rushed to his side.

"Okay, that does it. Soldier, your campaign is over. I'm sending you back to headquarters." He struggled and tried to get up, but I held him down. "Drover, the pain has clouded your mind. Listen to me. You can't go on! I'm ordering you to go home! I will not lead a wounded dog into combat."

He let out a groan. "Ohhhh! I don't want to be a weenie!"

"You're not a weenie, son, and this isn't your fault. Any dog who says you're a weenie will have to answer to me. Can you walk?"

"Well, I guess I can try." I helped him to his feet and watched as he took a few pitiful steps. It almost broke my heart to see him like this, a husk of his normal self. "I think I can make it, even if I have to crawl."

"Drover, I've never seen such a display of bravery. You've become an example for all of us in the Security Division."

"Gosh, no fooling?"

"Yes, and when this campaign is over, it will give me great pleasure to recommend you for the Order of the Double Cross. Well, good-bye, brave comrade. If fate is kind, we'll see each other down the road."

I whirled away from him before my emotions could get out of control.

# CHAPTER EIGHT

# A Mysterious Voice
# in the Fog

Without question, it was one of the most emotional moments of my whole career.

And this next part will really grab you. When we parted company, I heard Drover say, "I just hope I can live with the guilt!" Pretty touching, huh? You bet. I mean, right to the very last, the little guy was tormented that he had to leave the front lines.

And me? I felt like a scrounge. I mean, how many times had I accused him of being a weenie, a chicken liver, a half-stepper, and a slacker? Now my words came back to honk me and I felt nothing but shame and remorse. Tears stung my eyes as I stopped and took one last look at my . . .

HUH?

I couldn't believe it. Unless my eyes were playing tricks on me, Drover had made a miraculous recovery. I mean, the limp had vanished and he was now skipping and hopping and . . . gee whiz, chasing a butterfly!

I was thrilled and shouted, "Drover, great news! I'm changing your orders. You can rejoin your outfit and march with us into combat!"

He froze, stared at me for a moment of heartbeats, and then took off running as though he'd been shot out of a cannon.

"Drover, this way! You're running in the wrong direction! You've been cleared for action! You can return to your . . ."

He shrank to a dot on the horizon, then vanished. Had he misunderstood my order? Or had he . . . I cut my eyes from side to side and my mind tumbled.

THE LITTLE FAKER!

Never mind. I'll say no more about this shameful chapter in our ranch's history.

Yes, I will. Remember all that stuff about Drover's bravery and heroism? Garbage, total garbage, and I'd be grateful if you'd take a dark pen and mark out all those passages. No, even better, cut them out with a pair of scissors and throw away the scraps.

You want the real story on Drover? He's a little WEENIE and he'll always be a little weenie, and I can't believe I ever . . .

Skip it. Let's move on to something else. I mean, I had more important things to think about, right? I was on a special-ops mission to locate a wandering bird dog, a mission that would take me right into the heart of country that was controlled by wild tribes of cannibals. For that, I would need all my wits and instincts, and I had no time to be distracted by . . .

*I couldn't believe I'd fallen for Drover's Blowout Scam!* How many times had he pulled that same trick on me? Dozens of times. Hundreds of times.

You know my biggest problem? My biggest problem is that I'm too nice, too trusting, too kind. I have this heart of gold, see, and dogs like Drover take advantage of it. He ought to be living with someone with a heart of *granite*, but never mind.

Where were we? I have no idea. You see what he does to me? The mutt is a full-goose bozo, a lunatic, and it really torches me when . . .

Plastic, that's what we were discussing. Growing up, I chewed bones and sticks, sometimes an old shoe if I could find one, but somehow I missed out on the joy of chewing . . .

Forget plastic. Plato, that's where we were. I was on a mission to . . . you know, this was pretty crazy, me going into Cannibal Country to look for a bird dog who had caused me nothing but grief. And this wasn't the first time I'd been called upon to save his skin.

But don't forget, this time I had been promised a reward. Wow. Think about it. The lovely Miss Beulah had promised to ditch the pest, once and for all, and with Plato out of my life . . . heh heh . . . I could see nothing but roses in the future.

Every game has a winner and a loser. In the game for Beulah's heart, Plato had won his share, but now he was fixing to lose the Big One. Heh heh. Too bad, but who's going to lose sleep over a brokenhearted bird dog? Not me.

Does that sound cold-blooded? Too bad. That's my biggest problem, you know. My line of work has made me so tough and hard that I have no sympathy for slackers, losers, bird dogs, or cats. Sometimes it bothers me, knowing that I have this plate of steel that covers my deeper feelings, but it comes with the job. If you go into Security Work, you have to be tough.

But of course I still had to find the dummy,

and that wasn't going to be a cakewalk under the bird's nest. Don't forget that I was heading toward canyon country, which consisted of several square miles of deep canyons, far from civilization and crawling with heartless cannibals.

There are no maps or charts of canyon country. When we dogs venture into this hostile region, we leave the easy life behind and hark back to the oldest, deepest instincts of our doggie ancestors, those old ones who lived and died by their noses, ears, eyes, and wits. Out there in the wilderness, a dog eats what he can catch, drinks water that he digs out of the hard ground, and takes shelter wherever he can find it.

Most of your ordinary mutts would never set foot in such a place. Me? Actually, I kind of enjoyed . . . okay, maybe I felt a wee bit uneasy as I moved deeper and deeper into the . . . as the silence of the place closed around me and the walls of the canyons rose higher and . . .

Anyways, as I was saying, it suddenly occurred to me that I had forgotten about several important meetings I needed to attend. No kidding. I hadn't thought to, uh, check my calendar, don't you see, and, well, these meetings never quit. Ha ha. If we're not meeting about the ranch budget, we're setting policy on . . . well, Rabbit Control or postal employees or you name it.

So, yes, the office was calling me back, and with a heavy heart, I checked the location of the sun to plot my course back to . . . hmmm, the sun had disappeared behind a bank of clouds and . . . you know, we have about fifteen canyons up there and every one of them looks pretty muchly like the rest of them . . . rough, deep, spooky . . .

Fog? Who had ordered fog? This was exactly the wrong day and time for a dense, choking, insputterable . . . who expects heavy fog in the Texas Panhandle? We're in a semi-arid region. We get twenty-one inches of rain per year, and sometimes less than that. Fog belongs in places that have green grass, coastlines, foghorns, seagulls, and jellyfish.

By George, all at once I had the strangest feeling that . . . gulp . . . WHERE WAS I!!! Standing inside a bubble of asparagus soup, that's where, and I couldn't see squat in any direction. This was ridiculous! How can a cowdog get lost on his own ranch?

Bird dogs get lost because they have a great nose wired up to a flea's brain. They get lost because a great nose can lead a dog into places a

flea's brain can't get out of. They get lost because they are dumber than a box of rocks, but cowdogs never get lost on their own . . .

Gulp.

I reached for the microphone of my mind. "Data Control, this is Foxbat 36. We're having a little trouble with our GPS readings. Could you help us out with that? Over." I listened to static on the receiving unit. I spoke louder into the mike. "DC, we have a problem. We seem to have lost our satellite link. Could you crank up the power? Over."

I strained to hear the faint message: " . . . lose thirty pounds in just one week, guaranteed! Ugly fat melts away from hips, thighs, and jowls. After just one week of eating plastic . . ."

I slammed the mike back into its cradle and stared into the rolling void of fog that had become my prison cell. I was all alone on this deal and had lost all contact with the outside world. In my whole career, I had never felt so . . .

"Help!"

Huh? Did you hear that? Maybe not, because you weren't there, but I heard it—a voice of distress calling out from somewhere in the depths of the fog. I fine-tuned my Earatory Scanners and homed in on the signal. Moments passed, then . . .

"Help!"

Holy smokes, there it was again! At that point, I activated our sending devices and began broadcasting on our Emergency Frequency.

Would you like to see a transcript of the conversation? It's highly classified material, but ... oh well, I guess it wouldn't hurt to go public with it. Stand by.

## NATIONAL SECURITY AGENCY
## RECEIVING STATION
### Fort Frijole, Arizona

### Eyes Only! No Ears, Toes, or Ankles!

HANK: "Hello?"

VOICE: "Hello!"

HANK: "Are you there?"

VOICE: "Yes! How about you?"

HANK: "I'm here, yes."

VOICE: "Great! Say, this fog is really something, isn't it?"

HANK: "Roger that. Who are you?"

(Long Pause)

VOICE: "Listen, it makes me uneasy to speak to someone I've never met."

HANK: "Right, me, too. Maybe we should introduce ourselves."

VOICE: "Great idea. You go first."

HANK: "Why don't you go first?"

VOICE: "Well . . . I don't even know your name."

HANK: "Look, tell me yours and I'll tell you mine!"

VOICE: "Can you give me a minute to think about that?"

HANK: "Sure."

(Three-Minute Pause)

HANK: "Hello? Are you still there?"

VOICE: "Right, still here."

HANK: "What are you doing?"

VOICE: "Well . . . not much. How about you?"

HANK: "I'm waiting for you to identify yourself."

VOICE: "You know, I'd rather not."

HANK: "Okay, tell me this. Are you a coyote?"

VOICE: "Oh no, not at all. How about yourself?"

HANK: "I'm not a coyote."

VOICE: "Do you have any proof of that?"

HANK: "I'm not a coyote! Come over and look."

VOICE: "Why didn't I think of that? Where are you?"

HANK: "I have no idea. Where are you?"

VOICE: "You know, I've been wondering about that."

HANK: "How long have you been wherever you are?"

VOICE: "I've been wondering about that too, actually."

HANK: "Okay, describe your location."

VOICE: "Sure, you bet. I see dirt and ... fog."

HANK: "That's terrific, dirt and fog."

VOICE: "Oh, and I think I'm in a sort of cave."

HANK: "Cave? What makes you think so?"

VOICE: "Well, because I came into a cave and I haven't left."

HANK: "Can you give me a description of the cave?"

VOICE: "Well, it's ... it's a hole ... with a dirt floor."

HANK: "All holes have dirt floors."

VOICE: "You know, that's a great point. I hadn't thought of that."

HANK: "Wait a second. By any chance, are you a bird dog named Plato?"

VOICE: "Why . . . yes! But how did you know?"

HANK: "Incoherent rambling."

VOICE: "Excuse me?"

HANK: "Never mind. It's me, Hank the Cowdog."

VOICE: "Hank! By golly, what a small world!"

HANK: "It's bigger than you think, pal."

**END OF TRANSMISSION**
**Please Destroy Immediately!**

# I Find the Birdly
# Wonder

Okay, there it is and now you know the scoop. My Search and Rescue Mission had been a tremendous success, and against incredible odds, I had managed to find the Birdly Wonder in a deep canyon in the densest of fogs. All indications were that he was still alive and babbling.

At this point, it appeared that only one problem remained: neither one of us had any idea where we were. Search and Rescue missions always work better when someone knows where he is, don't you see, and, yes, this presented us with a few challenges. But I soon learned that we had a second problem, one I hadn't expected.

Through the fog, I heard Plato's voice again. "Hank, what are you doing out here?"

"Well, what do you think? I came to save you, at the request of a certain lady dog named Beulah."

"Oh dear."

"Come back on that?"

"Hank, we need to talk."

"We are talking."

"I know, but . . ." His voice trailed off into silence.

"Hello? Plato?"

"Hank, I can't see you right now."

"Well, I can't see you either, so maybe we should try to find each other."

"No, you don't understand. What I mean is . . . I don't want to see you. And I don't want you to see me."

*"What!"*

"Hank, try to understand. I haven't eaten in three days. I've shrunk down to skin and bones, I look horrible. I'm a bag of ribs, Hank."

"Yeah, and do you know why? You walked away from an easy job, a soft bed on the porch, and a dog bowl heaped with food . . . to chase birds! That's the kind of Dumb that has no name, pal."

"I know, and that's why we can't meet. I'm so ashamed of myself! Hank, go back, don't waste your time with me. I'm not worth it."

Well, he was right about that. He wasn't worth it, but I'd come a long way to find the dingbat and I didn't intend to leave without him. But to find him in the fog, I would have to use trickery. I studied on it and came up with a plan.

"Okay, Plato, have it your way. We won't meet."

"Thanks, Hank, I was hoping you'd understand."

"But do me one favor."

"Anything, you name it."

"Tell me what causes a bird dog to leave home and start roaming."

For several long moments, he said nothing, then . . . "All right, Hank, I'll try. It's the least I can do."

By now, you've figured out my plan. See, the mutt was a jabbermouth, and I figured I might as well use his jabbering as a homing bacon. Beacon. A homing beacon, similar to the electronic signal that directs fighter aircraft back to their landing base in the dead of night.

If I could get him talking about his dreary little life, I could follow the sound of his voice and track him through the fog. Pretty awesome, huh? You bet.

He started talking. "Hank, all my life I've had this problem with . . . I think the term is 'wander-lust.' Is that the word?"

"It's your life, Plato, you choose the words."

"Good point. Hank, now and then, I'm seized by this irrational desire to stray, to pursue the . . . the Great White Quail."

I groped my way through the fog. "The Great White Quail?"

"Right. Maybe it's unique to the hunting breeds, I don't know. Hank, it's a lovely vision, an elusive dream that the next quail will be absolutely perfect, the archetype of all quail since the beginning of time.

"I dream of finding that perfect quail, Hank, and of stalking it through miles of tall grass, and then I see myself going on point, as rigid and graceful as a statue made of . . . bronze, I think, or maybe alabaster. Yes, alabaster, Hank, gleaming white alabaster."

By that time, I had found the limestone cave where he was roosting. When I caught my first glimpse of him, I had to bite my lip to keep from laughing—this spotted, stick-tailed bird merchant, shrunk down to a bag of bones, sitting at the edge of the cave, staring with dreamy eyes

into the swirling fog, and yapping his little heart out about his quest for the Great White Quail.

He never saw me coming, had no idea that I had tracked him down and was standing ten feet away from him. I decided to let him finish his True Confession.

A dark shadow passed across his face and his foppish grin disappeared. "But Hank, in my depths, I realize that my quest for the perfect bird has . . . well, social consequences. Take Beulah, for example. Hank, she's everything a dog could ever want. She's . . ." His eyes softened and a smile tugged at the corners of his mouth. "I can see her eyes even as we speak, and that long collie nose that expresses . . . well, the dignity of her breed. And the smile that tells us so much about the soul within. Hank, she's the perfect woman, the perfect dog!"

He blinked his eyes and scowled. "Hank, sometimes when I'm off on a crusade, I awaken in the night and wonder . . . why did I leave the perfect woman and go looking for the perfect quail? You can't imagine how much anguish this has caused me!" His head sank down on his chest and he heaved a sigh. "And I have no answer. There it is, Hank. Now you know my story. Thanks for trying to help. You can leave now."

"Not just yet, Plato. There's more to this story than you thought."

When I stepped toward him, he looked as though he had seen a ghost. His ears stood straight up and his jaw dropped three inches. "Hank! But I thought ... you tricked me!"

"That's right, pal, I tricked you. As soon as this fog lifts, I'm taking you back home."

He dropped to the floor of the cave, covered his eyes with his front paws, and began moaning. "No, I won't go! I'm a failure, I can't face the shame and disgrace!" He whimpered and sniffled for a long minute, then peeked out from behind his paw. "You don't understand any of this, do you? It must sound crazy."

"Yes, as a matter of fact, it sounds as nutty as a pecan tree."

"I guess cowdogs don't have any of these wild compulsions."

"Apparently not." For some reason, my mouth began to water and I found myself ... well, glancing around the cave. "You don't have any plastic in here, do you?"

Plato uncovered his other eye and stared at me. "Plastic?"

"Right. You know, toys, milk jugs, bread bags,

garden trowels . . . anything made of plastic."

"I don't think so, but why do you ask?"

"No reason, just curious." My mouth continued to water. "Are you sure there's no plastic in here? I mean, it doesn't have to be huge, just something made of . . . Why are you staring at me?"

"Sorry." There was a moment of silence. "Hank, what's the big deal about plastic?"

"I'm dying of boredom, that's all. For thirty minutes I've been listening to you blabber about birds and . . ." I began roaming the cave. "I need a chew! There must be something in here made of plastic."

"Hank, may I offer an observation?"

"No. Keep your trap shut. I've got to find some plastic!"

I stormed through the cave like a dog possessed. I don't know what had gotten into me, but all at once I had this wild craving for . . . Nerves, that was it, and everyone knows that when a dog gets antsy, he needs to chew something, right? It was perfectly normal behavior, but you can't expect a bird dog to understand anything normal.

What I found on the floor of the cave was dirt, a few rocks, an old packrat nest, two rabbit skulls, and . . .

HUH?

Near the back of the cave, my eyes fell upon a sight that sent such a jolt of electricity down my spine, it almost burned a hole in my tail.

Hang on to something solid. We've reached the scary part.

# Cannibals in
# the Cave!

I froze in my tracks, turned slowly, and crept back to Plato. He was frowning and sniffing the air. "You know, Hank, there's an odd smell in here. Have you noticed?"

I stuck my nose in his face and whispered, "How long have you been in this cave?"

"Well, Hank, I'd hate to guess. You know, the days run together, but I'd say maybe two or three days."

My eyes almost bugged out of my head. "Idiot! You've been in here for three days, and *you didn't notice two cannibals sleeping in the same room?*"

His mouth dropped open. "Cannibals? You can't be serious."

"Buddy, I'm serious. Look for yourself!"

He squinted his eyes toward the back of the cave, where Rip and Snort, the notorious coyote brothers, were stacked on top of each other, snoring away. Plato flinched. "Well, I hardly know what to say, Hank. You have to understand that my nose has been calibrated for quail."

"Yeah, and your brain has been calibrated for sawdust!"

"Well, Hank, that seems harsh, but I can understand your feelings. And I want you to know that this is very embarrassing." He swallowed a lump in his throat. "What do you suggest at this point?"

"Shhh, not so loud. I suggest we get out of here, while the getting is good."

At that very moment, Snort sat up and we got our first glimpse at his cold yellow eyes. They chilled me to the bone.

You know, if Plato and I had carried on that conversation in normal tones, I don't think Snort would have awakened up . . . awoken up . . . aweekened up . . . phooey. I think he might have stayed asleep. We made our big mistake in dropping our voices to a whisper.

See, your average coyote can sleep on train

tracks and never hear the train, but drop your voice to a whisper, move around on tiptoes, try to be sneaky, and BAMMO! He comes roaring out of a stuporous state with eyes wide open and fangs flashing.

And there was Snort in all his hideous cannibal glory. After beaming us that yellow-eyed glare for a moment, he rose to his feet and—bad luck for us—stepped on his brother's face. Rip shot straight up and rubbed his nose, and already he was in a bad mood.

Snort looked at us and growled, "Uh! What dogs doing in coyote cavement?"

I heard Plato draw a gasp of breath. "Hank, may I speak frankly here?"

"Might as well."

"To be perfectly honest, I'm terrified of coyotes." He crept around and hid behind me. "You do the talking, Hank, and believe me, I'll stand behind everything you say."

"Yeah, I can see what you're standing behind. Me." I tried to hide the quiver in my voice and flashed the brothers a broad smile. "Rip, Snort! By George, it's great to see you again! How was the Fourth of July? Big celebration, I guess—lots of kinfolks, fireworks for the kids, huh?"

They stared at me and didn't move a hair. I had to keep talking. "Hey Snort, did you hear the story about the cannibal who died and went to heaven? Ha ha. Oh, you'll love this one! Want to hear it?" No emotion, not a sound. "Okay, maybe some other time. Listen, what do you guys think of this weather? What a fog, huh? Okay, you've been asleep, so maybe . . ."

Snort's voice came like the rumble of a volcano. "What dummy dogs doing in coyote cavement?"

My mouth had become so dry, I could hardly squeak . . . speak. Actually, my mouth had become so dry that squeaking was about all I could do. "Snort, I had a feeling that you'd be wondering about that, and I can assure you that I can explain everything. Honest."

The silence was poisonous. I had no idea how to explain *anything*, least of all what we were doing in his cave. I plunged on. "Okay, Snort, here's the story. I hiked all the way up here from headquarters to . . . to make you a deal."

"Uh. What deal?"

"Snort, do you know what you guys really need?"

"Guys need good grub, big yummy, oh boy."

"That's not what you need. What you need,

what you really need is . . . a bird dog. See, I'm willing to loan you my bird dog for a couple of hours. Pretty awesome, huh?"

Behind me, I heard Plato gasp. "Hank, could we have a word?"

"Shhh, I'm working on a plan to save our skins."

I turned back to Snort, who gave his head a shake. "Brothers not want bird dog. Bird dog too skinny, got too many bones for being good yum-yum."

"Right, but that's only if you plan to eat him. See, most folks don't eat their bird dogs. No kidding."

The brothers exchanged puzzled glances. "What most folks do with bird dog?"

"Well, bird dogs are experts at hunting birds, you know, pointing and fetching, stuff like that. You like to eat quail?"

Their tongues shot out of their mouths and mopped their lips. "Brothers eat quail pretty good."

"Well, there you are. In two hours, old Plato could find you a nice mess of quail."

Snort scowled. "Coyote cavement messy enough without quail mess."

"Right, but you've missed the meaning of 'mess.' See, a mess of quail actually means a *bunch* of quail."

Snort gave me a blank stare. "Bunch of quail make feathers everywhere, mess up coyote cavement even more so. Rip and Snort not give a hoot for messy bird mess."

Communicating with these thugs had always been a problem, and I could see that this conversation was leading nowhere. I shrugged and gave them a pleasant smile.

"Well, that settles it, Snort. I thought you guys might want to borrow my dog, but I guess that isn't going to work out, so . . ." I poked Plato in the ribs and began edging toward the mouth of the cave. " . . . so we'll just, you know, run along. Great seeing you again, and tell the family hello."

I turned toward the outside and . . . huh? You know, coyotes sometimes appear to be slow and lazy, and sometimes they *are* slow and lazy, but now and then they're seized by a burst of ambition and can move very rapidly.

That's what happened here. In the blink of an eye, those big lugs shot across the cave and were standing between us and the great outdoors—blocking the exit is what they were doing.

They gave us toothy grins and Snort said, "Ha

ha! Two dogs not leave so berry fastly. What else bird dog do besides make big quail mess?"

"Well, I . . . Snort, we really need to be getting back . . ."

Suddenly, he roared and pounded his chest. "Two dogs not leave!"

"Okay, fine, but you don't need to screech."

Snort slouched toward me and brought his toothsome mouth next to my face. "Snort screech when Snort want to screech." He opened his jaws and roared right into my face, blowing my ears straight out on my head. "What Hunk-dog say about that, huh?"

"Well, I'd say . . . what the heck, I guess we can stay awhile."

Snort flashed an evil smirk and pointed a paw at Plato. "Rip and Snort ready for singing. Bird dog know how to sing?"

I turned to Plato. "Okay, pal, here's our chance. Can you sing?"

Plato's eyes had glazed over. When he opened his mouth to speak, here's what came out: "Muh muh muh muh . . . help!"

I turned back to the brothers. "There you go. Did you hear that?"

"What means, 'Muh muh help'?"

"It means . . . Snort, bird dogs have their own unique language, don't you see, and . . ."

"Coyote not give a hoot for antique language! What means, 'Muh muh help'?"

By this time, I was sweating bullets but I had to plunge on. "It means that, yes, Plato can sing. He loves to sing and has a wonderful voice. Why, back home, he's known as the, uh, Wolf Creek Canary. No kidding."

The brothers nodded and grinned. "Uh! Rip and Snort ready for big song. Bird dog canary lead singing, ho ho!"

"Lead the singing? No problem. Hey, this guy's a trained, certified *choir director,* and he would dearly love to lead us in a song, right, Plato?"

You won't believe this. When I turned to the Quail King, his eyes rolled up into his head and he FAINTED! Yes sir, wilted and swooned to the floor like a wet mop. I was left stunned and speechless.

Meanwhile, the brothers were getting restless. "Uh. How come singing-canary bird dog fall down? Coyote brothers ready to sing song right now, 'cause Rip and Snort berry greater singest in whole world, oh boy!"

I was running out of ideas. "Hey, listen, guys,

he's . . . he's had an attack, no fooling. Sometimes he faints."

Their grins turned nasty, and Snort bellowed, "Rip and Snort wanting to sing pretty quick, or maybe beat up dummy dogs and break face!"

I turned back to Plato. "Moron! Wake up, you have to lead the singing!"

He moaned and fluttered his eyelids. "Help! Is this a movie? Where am I?"

"This is not a movie and we're about to be mugged by cannibals! Can you sing?"

He blinked his eyes and glanced around. "Sing? Are you serious?"

"Look at those two cannibals and tell me if I'm serious."

He turned toward the brothers and flinched. "Yipes! You're serious. But Hank, there's a problem." He leaned toward my ear and whispered, "I can't sing!"

"Oh yeah? Well, you're fixing to learn. You're not only going to sing, you're going to direct the choir."

Pretty scary, huh? I mean, it was good news that the brotherhood had singing on their minds instead of eating, but I had advertised Plato as a song leader and he had just informed me that he

couldn't sing, much less direct a choir of cannibals.

It wasn't looking good, and it got worse. All at
once Plato began wheezing, gasping, and turning
blue in the face.

Yipes!

# CHAPTER ELEVEN

# We Release the Anti-Cannibal Toxin

I turned to the gasping bird dog and screamed, "Now what?"

"Stress, tension, nerves! Can't breathe!"

"Oh yeah? Well, see if this helps." I grabbed him by the throat and shook him so hard, his eyeballs almost popped out of his head. "Is that better?"

"Yes!" he squeaked. "I think I can do it." I released him and, sure enough, he seemed much better. "But Hank, I only know one song. Mother used to sing it to us pups."

"I don't care about your mother. What's the song?"

"It's called 'The Sunbeam Song.'"

"Oh brother!" I threw a glance at Rip and

Snort. They were laughing, belching, and slugging each other, doing the sort of things that good-old-boy cannibals do when they're having fun. "I'm not sure they'll go for it, but we've got to give it a shot."

"Hank, what if I mess this up?"

I draped a paw on his shoulder. "Plato, if you mess up, you won't have to worry about finding the Great White Quail, because you and I will be dead meat."

"That's a lot of pressure. You know, Hank, I don't do well under . . ."

I shoved him toward the cannibals. "They're all yours, pal."

Plato took a moment to compose himself, then turned a terrified smile toward the brothers. "Fellas? Eyes to the front, please. We're all going to join together and sing 'The Sunbeam Song.'"

The brothers stopped goosing each other and stared at him with open mouths. Then they broke out in a roar of irreverent laughter. Plato gave me a helpless shrug. "Now what?"

"Crank it up, son. They'll either join in or start tearing us apart."

Plato blinked his eyes, caught a quick gulp of air, and launched into his song.

## The Sunbeam Song

When I was a puppy, my mommy would say,
"Now, sweetie, I want you to know
That children and puppies should try to
    be nice,
So nice that you'll actually glow.

"When children show manners and courteous
    ways,
Remarkable things start to fly.
The clouds roll away, the sun shows its face,
And sunbeams race down from the sky."

    A sunbeam, a sunbeam,
    Mommy wants us to be sunbeams!
    When children show manners and
        courteous ways,
    Their sunbeams will brighten the day.

One morning I woke at a quarter to ten,
My mood was as dark as a crow.
I frowned and I pouted and looked out the
    door,
The world was all covered with snow!

But Mommy came over and whispered to me,
And urged me to squeeze up a grin.

I did, and by golly, the snow disappeared.
It melted from sunbeams within.

> A sunbeam, a sunbeam,
> Mommy wants us to be sunbeams!
> Bad weather's no match for a bright happy
>     grin,
> It's warmed by the sunbeams within.

This song has a moral, I'm sure you'll agree,
That happiness wins every time.
Our attitude makes the day better or worse,
And frowning is almost a crime.

We all have the choice of trying to be
Sunbeams or agents of gloom.
If you can't be wholesome and happy and
    bright,
You might as well go to your room.

> A sunbeam, a sunbeam,
> Mommy wants us to be sunbeams!
> If all you can do is contribute to gloom,
> You might as well go to your room.

Well, Plato managed to get through the song
without fainting or making any serious musical
blunders, and I'll admit that I was surprised. I

mean, when you're working with bird dogs, you don't expect great things, right?

But I was even more surprised when I glanced over at the cannibal brothers. I had thought they might make some kind of response—clap, cheer, hoot, jeer, laugh, ridicule, snarl, something—but they just sat there like a couple of logs, staring at the ground with vacant eyes.

Plato and I exchanged puzzled glances, and he said, "You know, I'm not sure they liked the song. Are they always so subdued?"

"Coyotes are never subdued."

"Yet they seem very quiet, don't they?"

"Yes, and that worries me. I'd better check this out." I walked over to Snort and moved my paw back and forth in front of his glazed eyes. No response. "Uh . . . Snort? Hello? Anybody home? Yoo-hoo?" At last he looked at me. "Hi there. Well, Plato did his song, so I guess we'll be running along."

"Dummy dogs not going nowhere, stay in coy-ote cavement forever."

"Forever? Gee, that's a long time, and we really need to be . . ." I looked closer at his face. "Snort, I don't want to alarm you, but you don't have a healthy color. In fact, your face looks . . . green."

He gave me a menacing glare. "Snort not give a hoot for color of face."

"I know, but . . . green? It's unnatural. It makes me wonder . . ."

His lips rose, exposing two rows of shark teeth. "Hunk-dog shut stupid mouth about green! Rip and Snort not give a hoot for color, only give a hoot for . . ."

My goodness, he burped.

"Bless you."

"Hunk shut trap!"

"Yes sir. Sorry I mentioned it." I rejoined Plato at the rear of the cave. He was waiting to hear my report. "Well, they won't let us go and Snort seems to be in a real bad mood. It's not looking good."

Plato scowled and studied the brothers, who hadn't moved an inch and were still staring, wooden-eyed, at the floor. "You know, Hank, they seem to be turning . . . green."

"Right, and when I mentioned that, Snort told me to shut my mouth."

"Green doesn't seem natural, does it?"

"Right, and he didn't want to hear that either."

"Hmmm." Plato rubbed his chin with a paw. "You know, Hank, if I were guessing, I'd say they were . . . sick."

I stared at him as a whirlwind of thoughts moved across my mind. "Sick! That's it! Don't you get it? They're cannibals and their bodies have no resistance to wholesome music! Your song was so wholesome, it's making them sick!"

Plato blinked his eyes. "You really think so?"

"Yes, and you know what else? I just figured out how we're going to bust out of here." I whispered my plan in his ear.

"You think it might work?"

"I know it'll work! Sunbeams, smiles, manners, happiness . . . those things are all *anti-cannibal*! One more chorus should push them over the edge. Are you ready?"

"I suppose, but in all candor, Hank . . ."

"Dry up and sing!"

We turned toward the brothers and belted out another chorus of "The Sunbeam Song." They responded immediately, as though we had just uncorked a vial of deadly toxins and released them into the air. A look of horror came into their eyes, and they began gasping and gagging and covering their ears.

They dragged themselves up to a standing position and weaved back and forth on legs of mush. By the third line of the chorus, their color had turned from light green to a darker, alarming shade of green, and the lights had gone out inside their eyes. On the last line of the chorus, their heads were moving up and down, and I heard Snort let out a groan.

"Uh! Wholesome song make Snort sicker than horse!"

And with that, he bolted away, leaped off the edge of the cave, and vanished into the fog. Rip stumbled around in circles for another moment, his eyes crossed and green foam dripping from his mouth, then he too went flying out of the cave.

There followed a moment of eerie silence, the kind of silence that only a heavy fog can produce, but it was soon shattered by the thunderous sounds of two poisoned cannibals . . ."Calling Earl and Ralph," as the cowboys say.

"Earl! Ralph! Earl! Ralph!"

Plato shook his head in amazement. "Honestly, Hank, this is the oddest thing I ever saw." He grinned. "But, you know, it worked."

"It sure did. Now let's get out of here, before the Anti-Cannibal wears off. When it does, those guys are going to be mad enough to eat rocks."

We dashed to the ledge and went flying out of the cave. Since the brothers had gone to the left, we went to the right and headed . . . well, south, I hoped, but I really didn't care, as long as we did-n't meet any cannibals in the fog.

I hated to make this trip at Turbo Speed, but the thought of being recaptured by the brothers solved any questions I had about . . . BAM . . . run-ning into rocks or . . . BAM . . . cedar trees in the fog, and yes, we had a few confrontations with solid objects in the murk.

But after we'd run a quarter-mile or so, the fog suddenly lifted and we set a Speed Course that would take us back to the ranch.

When we saw ranch headquarters in the dis-tance, Plato slowed to a walk, then stopped. "Hank, I must ask you something. Will we be see-ing . . . Beulah?"

"If she's still around, yes."

He hung his head. "I can't do it! I'm so ashamed of my behavior, running off again like a . . . like a featherbrained bird dog!"

I laid a paw on his shoulder. "Plato, I've got some good news and some bad news. The good news is that I promised Beulah I would bring you back alive, and I did. The bad news, as far as you're concerned, is that you're *out*."

He stared at me. "Out?"

"Right. I can't think of a nicer way to put it. You are now Beulah's former bird-dog boyfriend."

"You mean . . ."

"Yes. That's the deal she made with me: if I brought you back safe, she'd make me Number One in her life. Now you're free to chase the Great White Quail and stay gone as long as you want."

He was stunned. "Hank, I must tell you something. There really isn't a Great White Quail. It's just an illusion, a compulsion, a crazy dream. I realize that now."

"That's right, pal, and it cost you a girlfriend. Plato, from the depths of my heart, I can say that you are the dumbest dog I've ever known." I gave him a pat on the shoulder. "Now, if you'll excuse me, I have a date with a lady, and you can run along. Good-bye."

"Good-bye, Hank. No hard feelings. I got what I deserved."

He turned and walked away with his nose and tail dragging the ground. For a moment, I felt a sting of sadness, but then a picture of Beulah popped into my mind and, well, somebody has to lose. Better him than me, right?

# CHAPTER TWELVE

# The Pledge of No Plastic

Okay, it was sad, but how many tears can you shed over a soap opera that stars a bird dog? Not many. He got exactly what he deserved and he'd said so himself.

The Great White Quail. How dumb is that?

But just because Plato's life had been splattered like a bug on a windshield didn't mean that I was going to worry about it. No sir, I had big things waiting for me. Just think about it. For years I had courted Miss Beulah with every trick in the book, and now, at last, I had her all to myself!

I went skipping into headquarters, so happy that my feet hardly touched the ground. "Beulah? Yoo-hoo, Miss Beulah? The conquering hero hath returned from his journey and is ready to collect the rent, as you might say."

I didn't find her at the machine shed. Had she gone back home? Surely not. We'd made a deal and she would be waiting for me, right? Of course she would.

I checked several other places and was beginning to feel some irritation. I mean, she should have been waiting and watching, so that she could rush into my arms the moment I entered ranch headquarters. Isn't that the way it's supposed to work when the hero returns? Of course it is.

But then I saw her down by the yard gate, and fellers, my heart did flips and cartwheels. Even at a distance, I could see the flame of love shining in her gorgeous collie eyes and . . . huh? Drover?

Little Buttinski was perched right beside her, wearing his patented silly grin and looking at her with an adoring gaze. You see? That tells us all we need to know about his so-called bad leg. The little faker had . . .

Oh well, no harm done. I was sure the runt had bored her senseless with his poetry. Heh heh. Actually, I couldn't have planned it better myself. A couple of hours of Drover makes great advertising for anyone else—ME, for example.

I went swaggering down to the gate. When

Drover saw me, he cringed and crept around be-hind Beulah. "Hank, I hope you don't think . . . we were just . . ."

"Never mind, son, I'll settle accounts with you later." I turned a pair of wolfish eyes toward the lovely Miss Beulah and wiggled my left eyebrow. "Howdy, ma'am. I'm back."

I was a little disappointed that she didn't come flying into my arms. Instead, she studied me with a level gaze. "Did you find Plato? Is he all right?"

"Yes ma'am, he is. To save the mutt, I had to whip half the coyotes in Ochiltree County. If the other half had shown up, it would have taken me another thirty minutes."

"Did you tell him . . . about us?"

"I did, yes."

"And how did he take it?"

"Well, he walked away with his tail dragging the ground and he probably thinks his heart is broken, but he'll get over it. This time next week, he'll be off on another crusade to find the Great White Quail."

She turned away from me. "Hank, I know I gave you my word, but I'm having second thoughts. It's about Plato, not me. The poor dear gets so distracted, he needs someone to look after him."

"Right. He needs to be put in a home, a kennel with all the other bird dogs in the world. Beulah, the mutt doesn't deserve you, and he even said so himself."

I heard her sniffle. "That sounds just like him, so kind, so humble."

"Oh brother! He has every reason to be humble. He's a nitwit."

She turned to me with pleading eyes. "Hank, please, I beg you to reconsider."

I showed her a frozen smile. "I will not reconsider. I won you fair and square, and I intend to collect my . . ." At that very moment, I noticed an object lying at Beulah's feet. "Drover, is that my garden trowel?"

He peeked his head out from behind Beulah. "I thought it was Sally May's."

"It used to be Sally May's, but I claimed it."

"Yeah, but you dropped it. I figured you didn't want it."

"What is my Priceless Plastic-Handled Garden Trowel doing out here?"

"Well . . . I thought it would make a nice present for Beulah."

I felt my eyes bulging. "What? You gave away my most treasured possession? Why, you little thief, give me that!" I made a dive for the trowel, but Drover got there first. He snatched it up and scampered away. "Drover, come back here, and that is a direct order!" He kept running, so I turned to Beulah. "Excuse me, ma'am, we've had a robbery."

Her eyes grew wide. "You're *leaving*, at a time like this? We're in the middle of a very important discussion."

She was right. I knew she was right, but she didn't understand the magnitude of Drover's crime. I began pacing. "Beulah, that trowel is priceless! It has a plastic handle."

"A plastic handle! What's wrong with you?"

My mind was swimming, I hardly knew what I was saying. "I don't know . . . but *I have to chew that plastic*!!"

She stared at me and pulled herself up to her full height. "Hank, I used to think that Plato was daffy about his birds, but *you* . . . *plastic*! This is absolutely crazy!"

"I know it seems that way, but . . . listen, I'll be right back, honest. You wait here, don't move." I went roaring up the hill after the Trowel Thief. "Drover, if you chew my trowel . . . !"

Behind me, I heard Beulah's voice. "I hope you

enjoy your trowel, mister, because when you get back, I won't be here!"

"Beulah, be reasonable! This will only take a minute."

"I will never pledge my heart to a dog who *chews plastic*! Good-bye!

"Drover, come back here!"

I knew she wouldn't leave.

I was pretty sure she wouldn't leave.

SHE LEFT!

I couldn't believe it! I mean, it only took me thirty-five minutes to catch the thief, place him under arrest, confiscate the stolen trowel, and chew the plastic handle to smithereens. When I rushed back to the yard gate, she was gone, and with her she had taken all my hopes and dreams of romance.

I was crushed. Smashed. Absolutely devastated. I wasn't sure I would ever be able to glue the pieces of my life back together again. That evening at sundown, I found myself alone in an empty office, thinking back on a love story that had turned to ruins, and wondering if . . . well, if I'd been partly to blame.

Actually, I wasn't alone in the office. Drover sat nearby, serving jail time with his nose in the corner. Desperate for warmth and companionship, I found myself talking to him.

"I still can't believe she walked out on me."

"Yeah, but *you* walked out on *her*."

"Drover, I was recovering my Priceless Plastic-Handled Garden Trowel. Oh, and thanks a lot for wrecking my life."

"Can I take my nose out of the corner?"

"No. I just don't get it. What do these women want?"

"Well . . . dogs who don't chew plastic, I guess."

I ran my gaze over the two thousand pieces of plastic in front of me, all that remained of the trowel's handle. "Do you suppose Sally May will notice that her trowel is missing?"

"Sure."

"Do you think there's a chance she'll suspect . . . well, us?"

"She'll suspect *you*. I can almost guarantee it."

I heaved a weary sigh and paced over to him. "I was afraid of that. Drover, this tragedy has forced me to look deep inside myself."

"I tried that once, but I couldn't see past my belly button."

"Please hush. I'm trying to tell you something profune."

"Sorry."

I ran my gaze around the office. "Drover, I'm beginning to think that I should give up chewing plastic. I mean, when you view it from a certain angle, it seems . . . well, a really stupid thing to do."

"Yeah, and it makes all the women mad."

"Exactly. It's not as loony as chasing birds, but it has caused me a mountain of grief. Drover, as of this moment, I suggest that all of us in the Security Division take a pledge never to chew plastic again."

"I already did that once."

"I know, it gets confusing, doesn't it? But this time, Drover, we must swear off plastic forever."

"Can I take my nose out of the corner?"

I gave that some thought. "Okay, for this solemn occasion, we'll let you out of prison. You're a free dog, and I hope you use your freedom wee-dem."

"What?"

"I said, I hope you use your freedom wisely."

I gave him a few moments to hop around and celebrate his release from prison, then we assembled the entire staff of the Security Division and administered the Pledge of No Plastic. After the day's tragic events, the words took on a whole new meaning. Losing Beulah had been a terrible experience, but I knew that it had left me an older dog, a wiser dog in every way.

Never again would I fall for the luster of plastic!

After the ceremony, we retired to our respective gunnysack beds and prepared for a night of sad dreams and maybe a little sleep. I had just fallen into the warm embrace of my beloved gunnysack bed, when I heard an odd rustling sound nearby. I turned my head and saw . . . I couldn't believe my eyes!

"Drover, do you see what I see?"

"Yeah. It's a plastic soda-pop bottle. It must have blown out of the trash barrel."

"Exactly. Are you thinking what I'm thinking?"

A crazy gleam had come into Drover's eyes. "Just one more time?"

Anyway, we, uh, dropped right off to sleep and almost nothing happened.

The rest of the story is that—sigh—Beulah went back to her bird-dog boyfriend. For weeks and days and hours, I could hardly function, so deep was the wound to my . . . whatever. But slowly and painfully, my broken heart healed itself, and I was able to return to my duties as Head of Ranch Security.

Have I stopped dreaming about the lovely Miss Beulah? No, and I never will, and one of these days . . . well, there's always tomorrow.

Oh, remember the stolen twuck? We stayed on the case for several months, but finally had to give it up for, uh, lack of evidence. As of this writing, nobody knows what became of Little Alfred's plastic twuck. It just . . . well, vanished without a trace. No kidding.

This case is closed.

The following activities are samples from *The Hank Times*, the official newspaper of Hank's Security Force. Do not write on these pages unless this is your book. Even then, why not just find a scrap of paper?

# Rhyme Time

When Hank runs into Rip and Snort, they call him HUNK. Suppose Hank leaves the ranch and looks for a new line of work. What could he do?

Make a rhyme using the name HUNK that would relate to his new job possibilities.

**Example:** Hunk drops coins in a wishing well for people. (**Answer:** Hunk PLUNK)

1. Hunk becomes a swimming pool bully.

2. Hunk measures Christmas trees for skirts.

3. Hunk opens a bathhouse offering Emerald Pond baths.

4. Hunk builds summer-school camp sleeping quarters.

5. Hunk sells a perfume made from this bad-smelling coyote love potion.

6. Hunk takes a class to become a Russian translator.

7. Hunk becomes a triathlete but never finishes the swimming part of the races.

8. Hunk starts collecting old cars.

# Coyote Decoder

For each letter in the message, find the symbol and then count clockwise the number of spaces after the symbol to find the right letter.

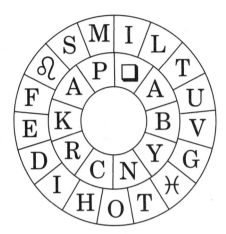

Use the coyote decoder (above) to unscramble the following quote from Rip and Snort.

" ⅗3 ♌6 ⬜4 ⬜7    ♌2 ⬜8 ⬜7 ⅗6    ⬜9 ♌4 ⅗6 ⬜4 ♌5 ⬜3

— — — —,    — — — —    — — — — —

♌8 ⬜6 ♌6 ⬜2    ♌1 ⬜1 ♌7 ⅗6    ♌4 ⅗4 ⅗1 ♌5 ♌4 ⅗6

— — — —.    — — — —    — — — — — —

⅗5 ⅗2 ♌8    ⅗7 ⅗2 ⬜6    ♌1 ⬜4 ⬜8 ⬜5 ⬜7

— — —    — — —    — — — — —. "

---

**Answer**:

"Hunk make plenty grub. Save little dog for snack."

# Word Maker

Try making words from the name below. Make up to twenty words with as many letters as possible.

Then, count the total number of letters used in all of the words you made. See how well you did using the security rankings below.

## HANK AND DROVER

_____    _____

_____    _____

_____    _____

_____    _____

_____    _____

_____    _____

_____    _____

_____    _____

_____    _____

_____    _____

### Security Rankings
**55-61** You spend too much time with J.T. Cluck and the chickens.
**62-67** You are showing some real security force potential.
**68-72** You have earned a spot on our ranch security team.
**73-** Wow! You rank up there as a top-of-the-line cowdog.

# Hank Quote

Unscramble the tiles below to reveal this Hank quote from *The Watermelon Patch Mystery*.

| | | | |
|---|---|---|---|
| R  O | I N T | T . | M E N |
| I N | L E T | Y O U | A W |
| P O | F L | M E | T  A |
| O U | I N T | | |

# Have you read all
# of Hank's adventures?

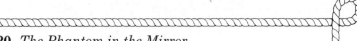

□ Yes, I want to join Hank's Security Force. Enclosed is $12.95 ($8.95 + $4.00 for shipping and handling) for my **two-year membership**. [Make check payable to Maverick Books.]

**Which book would you like to receive in your Welcome Package? Choose any book in the series.**

(#     )      (#     )
_____
FIRST CHOICE      SECOND CHOICE

                                     **BOY or GIRL**
_____
YOUR NAME                            (CIRCLE ONE)

_____
MAILING ADDRESS

_____
CITY                                STATE    ZIP

_____
TELEPHONE                        BIRTH DATE

_____
E-MAIL

Are you a □ Teacher or □ Librarian?

**Send check or money order for $12.95 to:**

Hank's Security Force
Maverick Books
P.O. Box 549
Perryton, Texas 79070

**DO NOT SEND CASH. NO CREDIT CARDS ACCEPTED.**
*Allow 4–6 weeks for delivery.*